MURDER AT THE ALAMO

A Cottonwood Springs Cozy Mystery - Book 5

BY

DIANNE HARMAN

Published by: Dianne Harman
www.dianneharman.com

Interior, cover design and website by
Vivek Rajan

ISBN: 9781090954176

CONTENTS

ACKNOWLEDGMENTS

To new readers: Thanks for picking this book up, and I hope you enjoy the read as much as I enjoyed the write.

To the readers who have enjoyed my books before: Thanks for your continuing support.

To all the people who worked so hard to bring this book about: Thanks for all your help.

To my family: Thanks for being my biggest cheering section.

And to Tom: For the hours and hours you've spent to make me a bestselling author!

Win **FREE** Paperbacks every week!

Go to <u>www.dianneharman.com/freepaperback.html</u> and get your FREE copies of Dianne's books and favorite recipes immediately by signing up for her newsletter.

Once you've signed up for her newsletter you're eligible to win three paperbacks. One lucky winner is picked every week. Hurry before the offer ends!

PROLOGUE

Mark Muller decided he'd head into work just a little earlier than usual. He'd been seeing one of the girls from the gift shop, and she usually got there early. He was hoping they could have a bit of alone time before they had to start their job duties at the Alamo. She made him feel something that no woman had ever done before. He wasn't sure what it was, but he definitely wanted to find out.

Working at the Alamo wasn't exactly Mark's dream job, but it did pay the bills and allow him to meet new people. All sorts of them came to San Antonio to visit the historic location, and while he'd been fascinated by the sense of history when he first started giving tours, now it was just like any other place to him.

Some said the Alamo was haunted by all the spirits of those who had died at that fateful battle, but Mark had never seen anything resembling a ghostly spirit. Did he sometimes get creeped out when he was alone there? Sure, but that could happen anywhere, and that didn't mean it was haunted. It really was just another old building, simple as that.

He sipped his coffee as he finished getting ready for the day and then quietly closed the apartment door behind him. He was behind on his rent again, so he didn't want his landlord, who lived a few doors down from him, to hear him leave. His landlord had threatened to evict him a few days ago. Mark knew he had a gambling problem. No, it was more than a problem, it was an addiction. It had become painfully obvious lately. Poker night with his friends had gone from a friendly game to him urgently trying to find a place where he could lay down a bet.

When he found the underground gambling ring online, he thought his luck would turn around. Instead, he'd lost his car, his savings, and his apartment would probably be the next thing to go. Most of his friends had stopped answering their phones when he called, afraid he was calling to ask them for a loan. A loan that never got paid back.

Mark didn't blame them. He was the one who'd dug himself into a hole, and now he needed to find a way out. He promised himself that once he won enough to pay back the people he owed, he'd stop gambling. But so far that hadn't happened. All he needed was for his luck to change just a little.

When he'd successfully made it outside without encountering his landlord, Mark slowly walked toward the bus stop. His hair had grown longer, because he couldn't afford a haircut, and dark blonde strands hung down in front of his face. He looked down while he was walking, so he wouldn't trip on the cracked and uneven sidewalk. He felt as though he should know the sidewalk by heart by now, but it never failed. If he didn't pay attention, he'd end up tripping and spilling coffee on himself.

He made it to the bus stop a few minutes before the bus arrived. He was grateful, because in his mind, there was nothing worse than running to catch the bus, only to miss it by a few minutes. Once it arrived, he climbed on board and flopped down in his usual seat. He spent the entire ride thinking about the situation he'd gotten himself into. Mark realized he'd been walking a tightrope for quite a while and something had to give.

He was seeing Zoey, who worked in the gift shop, but he'd secretly begun having an affair with Celine, who worked in the main office. It wasn't like he really wanted a relationship with Celine. It had started a little before his relationship with Zoey, and he figured it wouldn't last long, but it had. Between the gambling and juggling his social life between two women, he'd spread himself too thin. Maybe it was time to break it off with one of them. That would be the smart thing to do. But how could he choose? Both women were completely different from each other.

Zoey was only nineteen, seven years younger than Mark. She was full of energy and fun to be around. That's why he was heading into work early. Seeing her in the morning seemed to make his day go better. Like when the sun finally comes out after it's been cold and rainy for far too long. She was like a warm blast of comforting air after a long winter, and his life had definitely been a long winter. He knew he had strong feelings for her, but he was sure eventually she'd find someone closer to her age and leave him in the dust. Anyway, as sweet and kind as she was, he didn't deserve her.

And then there was Celine. Mark wasn't sure exactly how old she was. She was graceful, beautiful, and elegant. She had this air about her that just screamed confidence and that confidence carried over into the bedroom. He'd never been with an older woman before, but if this was what they were like, he was sold. She also had this way of making him feel like a puppy. She seemed to hold the leash, and if he wanted anything, he'd have to come to heel.

She didn't bend for him. Lying with her was almost like being chosen to bed a queen. You knew she was only allowing you to be with her on her terms. With the wave of her hand she could cast you out and not think twice about it. Which, of course, made Mark want to stick around. He knew he was in a dangerous dance, but he couldn't seem to stop the music.

Mark made his way to the front of the bus as it slowed down at his stop. He was still deep in thought when he walked through the employee entrance and made his way to the locker room. When he opened his locker, he noticed an envelope with his name on it that had been slipped inside his locker. He tore it apart and pulled out a folded piece of paper.

I know about Zoey. I think it's best if you find somewhere else to work, or you may find yourself in more trouble than it's worth. C

Mark sighed. So Celine had found out about Zoey. He knew he'd been playing with fire seeing two women at his place of work. But if Celine thought he was going to just quit his job to help her save face, she had another thought coming. He knew she was married, although she thought she'd been discreet by slipping her wedding ring off every day.

Maybe if she tried to force him to quit, he'd have to find her husband and let him know what she was up to. After all, if she'd been so casual about her affair with Mark, this probably wasn't the first time she'd stepped outside her marriage vows.

He tossed the note back in his locker before shoving his backpack inside it and slamming the door. It looked like it was going to be a very long and interesting Monday. Considering all the money he owed people, there was no way he could quit his job. He may not be making money hand over fist, but that didn't mean he could just throw himself to the wind and hope he found another job. No way. Although she was his superior, in charge of managing the tour guides and others, Celine couldn't fire him without a reason.

Mark left the locker room and went outside onto the Alamo grounds. The sun had just begun to rise higher in the sky and it looked like it was going to be a beautiful day. It was still fairly early, about 7:00 a.m., but the other employees who worked there would be arriving soon. The groundskeepers and a few others needed to make sure the place was in top condition before the visitors started arriving.

He pulled his phone from his pocket and sent a quick text to Zoey.

Meet me in our spot as soon as you get to work, he typed. He might as well come clean with her. If Celine had found out about Zoey and him, she'd probably jump at the chance to tell Zoey. Maybe if he just opened up about it, he could salvage his relationship with her. He realized when he'd seen the note that his feelings for Zoey outweighed anything he felt for Celine.

Long shadows played on the walkway he was headed down. The path was paved with stones and there was a rock wall on one side with arches that had what looked like metal gates attached to them. The wooden beams across the top of the walkway always made Mark feel as if someone was peering down at him. He shook off the feeling and continued walking towards where he'd asked Zoey to meet him.

That was when one of the shadows emerged from behind one of the arches and pointed something shiny and metallic at him. In the faint light, he couldn't see what it was, but it didn't matter. Instinctively he knew he needed to protect himself.

Whoever it was, they were dressed entirely in black. A black mask, shirt, pants, gloves. Even their shoes were black. He lunged at the person's hand, trying to wrestle whatever it was they were holding away from them. He struggled against them but as they wrestled, he knew the other person had the upper hand. They didn't seem to be stronger than he was, but Mark knew he wasn't exactly in top shape or conditioning. All the drinking he'd done while he sat around watching television hadn't helped him. The attacker had been prepared and was quickly gaining the advantage as they struggled and fought with each other.

Mark suddenly realized the metallic object he'd seen in the attacker's hand was a gun. The attacker held their grip on the gun and slammed Mark up against the rock wall. It stunned him, but not enough to make him give up the fight. This wasn't how the attacker had planned their meeting. They'd intended to step out, hold up the gun, and threaten Mark. Maybe then he'd come to his senses and do what needed to be done. They'd never pegged him for a fighter.

Mark pushed back, his hand now wrapped around the attacker's forearm. He squeezed as tight as he could, hoping it would hurt enough they'd drop the gun, but it didn't work. Suddenly a shot rang out. He didn't feel anything at first and he wondered if maybe he'd managed to turn the gun on his attacker. That was when he felt pain surge through his chest. One moment he felt nothing and then in the blink of an eye, a pain, so intense he could barely think, consumed him.

He felt like there was a lump in his throat, blocking his airway. He coughed, hoping to free the blockage, so he could breathe. Instead, something wet came out of his mouth and he felt as if he were choking. It was so hard to draw a breath and then he simply slid down to the ground, sure if he could just sit and cough a few times, he'd be okay. Looking down he saw blood spreading across his chest and then everything grew dark.

The attacker was shocked. This wasn't how it was supposed to happen. They looked around, afraid someone might come running at the sound of the gunshot, but thankfully, it was still early enough that hardly anyone was there. Time was of the essence. They had to get rid of the gun. If only Mark hadn't put up a fight.

It had been foolish to take a loaded weapon to confront him, but they thought they might have to fire a warning shot to prove they were serious. Instead, they hadn't even been able to say a word before Mark had lunged at them. Now he was lying in a pool of his own blood.

For a moment they considered whether or not they should help Mark, but they quickly dismissed the idea. Anyway, it looked like he was too far gone. If they tried to help and got caught, their life would be on the line. Instead, it was time to get away from the scene as fast as they could. They turned on their heel and took off, trying to put as much distance between them and the man they apparently had just killed as possible.

CHAPTER ONE

Brigid and Linc strolled through the airport, hand in hand. Brigid couldn't believe she was on her honeymoon with Linc. Truth be told, she'd been a little unsure whether or not she'd ever get the wedding itself planned. After the florist went missing, it had almost seemed like the universe was conspiring against her. Of course, everything eventually worked out, and the wedding had gone off without a hitch.

It had been a tough decision for the couple to decide where they wanted to honeymoon, but eventually they'd settled on San Antonio, Texas. Neither of them had ever been there before, and the place was rich with history and culture, which was something both Brigid and Linc loved. They'd searched online for all the popular places to visit and had planned out a loose itinerary for their stay.

"I don't know about you, but I'm really looking forward to this," Linc said as he squeezed Brigid's hand. "Just me and my beautiful wife. All alone together for a whole week and a half. It's going to be magnificent. Don't get me wrong, I love Holly to pieces, but..." he let his sentence dangle in the air between them.

"But it's hard to have a romantic evening with a teenage girl around?" Brigid asked with a grin, knowing she felt the exact same way.

"Something like that," Linc chuckled. "Like I said, don't get me wrong, I love her as if she was my own daughter, and I'm really glad you offered your home to her after her mother was murdered. She fits in with the two of us as if she really was our own."

"She definitely acts like you," Brigid said bumping Linc affectionately.

"What's that supposed to mean?" he asked in mock surprise.

"Exactly," Brigid said.

They stepped out of the San Antonio International Airport and took the sky bridge to the rental car center. Linc had reserved a car for them online and refused to tell Brigid what kind he'd gotten.

"When are you going to tell me what you rented?" Brigid asked. "You know I'm not a big fan of surprises."

"You like surprises just fine," Linc chastised as he gave the attendant his driver's license information. The young man disappeared around the corner. "But you don't like being left out of the loop. Trust me. You'll be happy. Just have a little patience, you'll see."

Brigid gave him a look that said she wasn't so sure, but she decided not to say anything. For the most part he was right. She knew she didn't like not being involved. That was one of the reasons she was always in the middle of some sort of a criminal investigation.

Once a real-life mysterious whodunit situation came along, she couldn't help but want to find the answer. Besides, how many times had she been the one who found the evidence that allowed the sheriff's department to catch the perpetrator and close the case? She felt her penchant for being involved had to be a big check in the plus category.

Even in the shade, the heat was intense. They'd known Texas in the summertime would be hot, but having just left Colorado, which thanks to the elevation was much cooler, the overwhelming heat was much thicker than Brigid had anticipated.

"I wish there was a breeze," she said as she pulled her shirt collar out and began to fan herself with her hand.

"Yeah, it is pretty hot," Linc admitted. "But I think you'll adjust okay. Once we're moving, it shouldn't be so bad. Sitting still in this kind of heat is the worst."

"I forget sometimes just how much you traveled before you settled down in Cottonwood Springs. Do you ever miss it?" Brigid asked, curious.

"Not really," Linc said. "I had some good times, but I usually traveled to the same places. Skiing, snowboarding, things like that. But I'm happy to trade it all in so I can spend the rest of my life with you. Besides, I think you wouldn't mind doing a little traveling now and then."

"True, but I think I'd rather go to a warm weather location rather than where they have skiing and snowboarding," she confessed.

Just then a red convertible pulled up next to them, and the young man from the car rental company hopped out and handed Linc the keys. Linc gave Brigid a huge boyish grin as he began to load their bags in the back. Brigid could tell he was trying to hide his excitement, but he was doing a poor job of it. He looked like a kid who'd been turned loose in a candy store.

"What is this?" Brigid asked, acting like she was shocked. She simply stood there gaping as she watched him. When she'd thought about what kind of vehicle Linc would reserve, this was totally not it. He never struck her as someone who'd want to drive something this flashy. Not that it wasn't a nice car, it was just a surprise.

"Well, after all, it is our honeymoon, right? Now's the time to pamper and spoil ourselves. We may as well ride around in style," he said as he moved to the passenger door and opened it for her. "Your chariot awaits, Mrs. Olson." He bowed down as though he were her chauffeur.

"Oh, Linc," she chuckled as she climbed in the car. After he shut the door behind her, she ran her hand along the immaculate interior. She wasn't sure exactly what kind of car it was, but it was beautiful. Thankfully, the interior wasn't leather, which she figured would have been incredibly hot in this climate. It was a nice tan color that was spotless.

She wondered if the car was new. Once she got over her shock, she had to admit she really liked it. But renting a car this nice had to have been a serious expense considering how long they were going to be in San Antonio.

"How much did this cost?" she asked after Linc climbed in and began pushing buttons to set the GPS on his phone.

"Don't worry about how much it cost," he said with a wink. "Just enjoy. We're here to have fun and live life a little differently than we would back home. This thing is nothing like my truck or your car."

"That's no joke," she said. Brigid eyed him with a suspicious look for a few moments before settling back into her seat. He was right. Maybe for once she should just sit back and relax. After all, it was supposed to be a vacation. And not just any vacation, her honeymoon. She didn't want to end up overthinking everything and not enjoy herself. It was a bad habit she was determined to leave behind.

As Linc followed the directions for exiting the airport, Brigid took a deep breath and leaned her head back against the head rest. With the top down and the breeze blowing her hair, she began to cool off and enjoy the warmth of the sun. She tipped her head back a little further, closing her eyes and letting go of all her worries. Now was not the time to focus on them.

This was just the beginning of a week and a half of rest and relaxation. No teenagers to worry about or her sister, Fiona, who was pregnant. No work responsibilities or any other mundane day-to-day stuff that always seemed to bog her down. No murders or missing persons. This was Linc's and her time together in their new roles as husband and wife.

Occasionally, Brigid opened her eyes to look around at the surrounding area. San Antonio reminded her of Denver. Most cities basically seemed to be fairly similar. They all had grocery stores, gas stations, things like that, all the usual trappings of the modern world when a bunch of people live in the same densely populated area. But there were subtle differences that reminded Brigid they were far from home. For one, the absence of the mountains in the nearby distance.

She'd grown accustomed to seeing them on the horizon, but now there were none. Not only had she grown up in Cottonwood Springs, but when she'd moved away, she'd lived in Los Angeles. The mountains surrounding the city were a presence there as well on a clear smog-free day. Here, the only thing on the skyline were the towering buildings of downtown.

"Looks like we'll be there soon," Linc said as he pulled her away from her thoughts. "Are you going to be in the mood to do anything this evening or do you want to just relax at the B & B?" he asked. "I can go either way."

"I'm not sure," Brigid admitted. "Maybe we can do something a bit more relaxing after we get checked in and settled? Sort of ease our way into things?"

"That's not a bad idea," Linc said, nodding. "We need to find out how far the River Walk is from our B & B. I saw online there are tons of places to eat there, and if it's nearby we could walk there to stretch our legs," he said with a smile. "We can also see what else they have to offer there."

"I'd like that," Brigid said easily. "Let's take our first night here in San Antonio nice and slow. Besides, most tours or anything else we planned to do will probably be wrapping up by the time we finish dinner."

Linc nodded. "Sounds like we have a plan for the evening then," he said as he reached across the seat and squeezed Brigid's hand. "By the way, I think I'm already in love with this car," he said.

"Oh?" Brigid asked. "You think you'd like to have a convertible back home?" she asked with a raised eyebrow.

"Can't you just imagine cruising through the mountains with the top down?" he asked. "Smelling those fresh pines and clean clear air. Nothing between you and nature. It would be an amazing experience."

"That would be nice," Brigid agreed. "But what about in the winter when it's below zero? Would you still want to cruise around in it then?" she asked.

Linc began to frown. "No, that doesn't sound like as much fun," he admitted. "But do you think we could keep it in storage in the winter?" he asked, brightening at the idea. He knew it wasn't practical, but he didn't care. Sometimes you had to do things that were impractical just to make life a little more fun.

"I think you need to slow down," Brigid laughed. "Let's not jump ahead of ourselves. Why don't we enjoy it while we're here and worry about everything else when we're back home?"

"Okay," Linc sighed. "Present moment, right?" They'd both been reading a book on mindfulness and had been doing their best to implement what they'd learned.

"Exactly," Brigid said as she turned to watch the scenery go by. "We have to stay in the present moment. Let our future selves worry about what happens in the future."

"Well then I think I need to buy my past self a drink," Linc said.

"Why's that?" Brigid asked with a curious look on her face.

"Because he had the good sense to meet you, of course. I owe that guy, big time. I'm not even sure if I could ever repay him." Linc grinned, but continued to watch the traffic in front of them.

"That's true," Brigid said as she raised her hand to his shoulder. She traced the edge of his ear with her finger, gently caressing the soft flesh. "I guess that means I owe him a big thank you as well," she said as she continued to play with Linc's ear. Her fingers trailed down to his neck and toyed with his hair.

"I think I better accept that one on his behalf," Linc said, his voice low and seductive.

"We'll see about that," Brigid purred. Slowly, she lowered her hand and moved back to looking out the side window. *Better to tease him and then leave him wanting more,* she thought. *Otherwise they might not ever make it out to dinner.*

"Now I can't wait for this evening," Linc said as they left the interstate, following the GPS's directions.

"Let's just get to the B & B first, tiger," Brigid said. "There's a lot to do between now and then."

CHAPTER TWO

"This is it," Linc said as he slowed down and pulled into a long driveway. The home was even more beautiful than the pictures online had shown. It was a large two-story house that looked as though it was straight out of a Civil War era movie.

The Silver Star Bed and Breakfast had tall white columns in front of it, a wraparound porch, a wide landing upstairs, with black shutters framing each window. Brigid could imagine the owner closing them over the windows for protection if a bad storm blew in, which wasn't unusual in this part of Texas.

The driveway led around to the back of the house where there was a small parking area and a large garage. The house, garage, and a gazebo were all painted white. The spring flowers that had been in the online pictures were all gone by now, but there were colorful plants along the edge of the B & B as well as in the back yard. The brick sidewalk which ran through the yard was well taken care of without a weed in sight. Brigid was impressed. From the attention to detail, whoever took care of the yard obviously did it as a labor of love.

"Wow," Linc said as he parked the car. "It almost looks like something from a movie or one of those architectural magazines. I wasn't expecting it to look this nice."

"Me, neither," Brigid admitted. "But now I'm really excited," she said with a grin as they climbed out of the car. She inhaled deeply as she looked at the large imposing trees along the edge of the yard that towered over everything. Only slivers of light snuck through, keeping the entire yard in the shade. They retrieved their suitcases from the trunk and walked up to the door.

"Come in, come in," a jolly voice called out as they approached the screen door, their feet making hollow sounds on the old wooden porch. Inside, the main door was standing wide open and they heard the whir of ceiling fans. Linc held the screen door open for Brigid and she stepped inside.

The main room was fairly large. There were two couches facing a tall, imposing fireplace constructed of smooth river rocks. The wooden floors had a high sheen that matched all the wooden doors and trim surrounding the antique white walls. Long hunter green curtains framed the tall windows and landscape photographs hung on the walls. Although it was masculine, it was still very inviting.

"Good afternoon," the older gentleman in the rocking chair said. His chair was tucked between one of the couches and the fireplace, making a nice little cozy area to enjoy a fire if there had been one. Brigid imagined he spent many nights sitting there in the winter when it was cold outside.

He slipped a bookmark into his book and set it down on a small round table beside him. The German shepherd next to his feet had pricked his ears up at attention when they entered the room. "May I help you?" he asked.

"We're Mr. and Mrs. Olson," Linc said as the man stood up to greet them. "We made a reservation online with you."

"Ah, yes," the older man said. "Do come in. I have your room all ready for you." He walked somewhat stiff-legged at first as he stretched his legs out. By the time he made it over to them he was walking normally. "Let me get your room key, and I'll show you to your room. My name's John. John Hawk. And this is Charlie," he said as he gestured toward the large German shepherd that had followed him over to where Linc and Brigid were standing.

They shook John's hand and scratched Charlie behind his ears. John retrieved a key from behind a desk that was tucked in a nearby corner. It was an old roll-top desk that looked as though it had served its purpose for many years. After collecting the key, John motioned for Brigid and Linc to follow him toward the stairs.

"You're the ones on your honeymoon, correct?" he asked as he began to climb the beautiful wooden staircase. It rose a short distance before stopping at a small square landing and then turned to the right before rising once again. The stairs creaked and moaned with age as they walked up them.

"Yes, sir," Linc said, nodding in agreement. "We were married just a few days ago."

"Beautiful. Just beautiful. Always love it when newlyweds come to stay with me. My wife, Francis, God rest her soul, always said it was good luck to have newlyweds come here," he said as he reached the top. "It's never been bad luck, so she must have been onto something there," he said with a wink. "How was the wedding?"

"Gorgeous. We had a small ceremony in our yard with just family and friends," Brigid said, "which was just what we wanted. Do you take care of the B & B by yourself?" Brigid asked as they reached the top of the stairs.

"That I do," John said. "I retired from the police force a number of years ago. This place keeps me going, otherwise I'd probably just sit on my behind and get fat," he chuckled. "Besides, it's nice getting to meet folks like you from all over." He stopped in front of a door at the end of the hall. The small brass plaque on it was engraved with the words "Red Suite." "Here you are," he said as he unlocked the door. He pushed it open and stepped to the side to allow Brigid and Linc to enter.

Brigid was amazed at how beautiful the room was. The walls were the same antique white as the rest of interior of the B & B. The ceiling, however, was a lovely deep shade of red. The duvet cover, as well as the throw pillows and curtains, all matched the red ceiling.

"It's gorgeous," Brigid said.

Charlie trotted into the room and curled up beside the bed.

"Come on now, Charlie. You know better. Out," John called.

"Oh, he's no trouble," Brigid said as she leaned over and scratched Charlie's back. He seemed to smile in response. "I have a big Newfoundland dog at home, so Charlie's not a bother."

"Well, I'll leave that to you," John said with a smile. "Feel free to boot him out if he gets in your way. He's a loveable guy, but sometimes he gets underfoot."

"Not a problem," Linc said as he moved to shake John's hand again. "He won't be any trouble at all. We're dog people."

John nodded. "If you need anything, just let me know. Feel free to look around, and if you'd like any suggestions on places to visit, I've seen them all." He moved away from the door, and they heard his footsteps on the stairs.

"So, what's your story Charlie?" Linc asked as he sat down on the bed. Charlie greeted him with a cold nose bump. "Strong, silent type, hmm?" Linc asked.

Brigid laughed. "I don't think you're going to get too much from him." Her stomach began to growl loudly. "How about if we find somewhere to eat and unpack later?" she suggested.

"Fine by me," Linc said as he stood up from where he was sitting on the bed. "I bet John can point us in the right direction. Let's ask him about River Walk and see if he thinks that would be suitable for what we're looking for tonight."

They left their bags on the bed and headed out of the room, Charlie hot on their heels. When they stopped to lock the door to their room, Linc noticed how well- behaved Charlie was.

"He seems to be extremely well-trained," he said as he watched the dog.

"You think so?" Brigid asked.

"Yeah, I get the feeling he knows a lot more than your average dog," he said as they headed for the stairs. Their new four-legged friend followed right beside them, as if he belonged there. When they reached the ground floor, they found John back in the rocking chair with his book.

"May we interrupt you for a moment to ask you a few questions?" Brigid said as they joined John.

"Sure, have a seat," he said easily. "It seems like Charlie really likes you," he said with a gentle smile.

"Has he been professionally trained?" Linc asked.

"Yes, he has. Good eye. He's retired from the police force, just like me. I guess both of us are a couple of old men. Of course, he's still young at heart." He gave the dog a pat on his side.

"We were thinking of heading to the River Walk, but wanted to make sure it wasn't a noisy place. We kind of wanted to have an easy first evening here and didn't want some crowded tourist attraction right off the bat," Brigid explained.

"The River Walk would be great for that. Plenty of places to choose from. There are lots of relaxed style restaurants there as well as fancier places, if that's what you're looking for. You can also walk along the river or take a boat ride," he said.

"That sounds great," Brigid said as she turned towards Linc.

"You can have dinner on one of the boats, if that's more your speed. They show you the sights while you're eating great food," John explained. "What else are you two planning on doing while you're here?"

"We want to go to the Alamo," Brigid began. "We're also planning on heading to the beach for a day."

John nodded. "Might as well, as long as you're this close."

"Otherwise we're pretty open," she said.

"Well, depending on what you're into, there's a lot to see around here like the Natural Bridge Caverns and the Japanese Tea Garden. The younger crowd isn't into the nature stuff that much, but I always enjoyed it," he offered.

"I didn't know about those," Brigid said. "Thank you."

"Anytime," John said. "It's been a while since I visited either of them, but I'm sure they're both still great. I think they've even added more to the caverns, like a zipline and things of that nature."

"That sounds more my speed," Linc said with a grin. "I tend to lean more towards the thrill-seeking stuff, while Brigid prefers the nature walks and things like that."

"Well then you may want to consider heading in that direction. I know there's a website that can give you a bit more information than I have. I'm sure you could also find out the prices and other information."

"Thanks," Brigid said. "Well, Linc. You ready to go to dinner?"

"I think so," he said as they stood up. "Thanks again, John."

"My pleasure. You two have a good evening," he said as they walked over to the door. Charlie took a few steps as if he wanted to join them and then sat down. He whined as they walked away.

"Charlie, behave," John chided.

Brigid turned around and smiled. "Oh, Charlie, you sweetheart. You have to stay here. I'm going out to dinner."

The dog seemed to understand her words, because he returned to his spot next to John and plopped down as if he were pouting.

"He's going to break my heart," Brigid said.

"He's not normally like this. He must really like you," John explained.

"Maybe one of these days I could take him for a walk, if you don't mind?" Brigid offered.

"Of course. I'm sure Charlie would really enjoy that," John said with a smile.

Brigid gave both John and Charlie a little wave before she and Linc headed out the door and to the car with food on their mind.

CHAPTER THREE

Brigid was delighted when they got to the River Walk. It seemed like an American version of Venice, Italy. Not that she'd ever been there, but she'd seen enough pictures to have a rough idea what it looked like, and this seemed pretty close. Colorful umbrellas lined one side of the river while the other side had trees, bushes, and lots of greenery. Stone arch bridges crossed the river in various places and boats moved along the water with ease.

"I don't know what I was expecting," Linc began. "But it wasn't this." They both paused for a long time to simply take in their surroundings. It was nothing like anything they'd ever seen before, and they definitely hadn't anticipated something like this in the middle of a city.

"I agree," Brigid said. "It's almost magical, isn't it? It's like we just stepped into some sort of fairy tale village."

Linc nodded as he put his arm around Brigid's shoulder. "Exactly. I'd feel like we were in some time travel thing if it wasn't for everyone dressed in modern clothes." They looked around for a few more minutes and then Linc turned towards Brigid and said, "So, where do you think we should eat? Do you want to see about dining on one of those boats?"

They watched as one floated by and heard the tour guide

explaining the area to the people on the boat. Everyone on board was listening intently as they floated by and took pictures. Brigid thought the boat ride looked amazing, but couldn't imagine eating on one.

"No, I think I'd be too distracted to eat. I can only imagine how pretty everything is when viewed from down on the water. I'd probably still have a whole plateful of food left when the ride was over. Let's find somewhere to grab a bite and then we can find out about the tours. I'd rather be able to see everything and take pictures."

"Fiona would love to see this place. She'll be furious with me if I don't take tons of photos for her to check it all out." Brigid didn't want anything to get in her way of experiencing San Antonio to its fullest, even something as simple as a meal. Besides, she knew she was a slow eater to begin with. Having distractions wouldn't help.

They began to stroll along the sidewalk, pausing at each restaurant to check out the atmosphere and the menus posted in front of them by the sidewalk. There were little coffee shops, loud cafes with live music, and several restaurants that were more on the fancier side. They finally stopped at a steak house that wasn't quite as formal as a few of the other places they'd seen, but was still a very nice upscale restaurant.

It had a definite Texas feel to it with paintings of horses and cowboys hanging on the wall along with other types of Western décor. The smells coming from inside the restaurant were mouth-watering. They looked at the menu that was outside the restaurant, and it appeared you could get everything from a juicy steak to a hamburger. It looked like it specialized in American food, with an emphasis on beef.

They stepped inside and the young lady at the hostess stand asked if they would like a table inside or outside on the waterfront.

"Outside, please," Brigid said. She turned to Linc, "As long as that's okay with you?"

"Whatever you want. I'm just here for the food," he said with a grin.

They followed the woman outside to where she seated them at a table under one of the umbrellas along the river. The sun had begun to move lower on the horizon, casting long shadows across everything. Strings of fairy lights lit up the area, giving it a romantic glow. Their waiter took their drink order and then left them to look over the menu.

"I don't know how I'm going to decide what to order," Linc said. "Everything looks amazing. There are so many items to choose from. How in the world do I choose?"

"I'm in the same boat over here," Brigid agreed. "I want to try a little bit of everything."

They continued to look over the menus before finally settling on some appetizers and entrees. The waiter came back and took their orders before leaving them alone again.

"This city is beautiful," Brigid said as she looked around. "It has a completely different vibe than any other place I've been."

Linc nodded. "I noticed it, too. It's not that it's overly modern. You're practically enveloped in history here, but there's also a young and vibrant feel to the place. It's kind of like the city itself is alive."

"Exactly! Even this area we're in right now. There's almost a tangible life force to everything. Plus, it's all just beautiful to look at," she marveled. "The stairways, the bridges, even the buildings. It's so full of character."

"We made the right choice in coming here," Linc said as he took a sip of his iced tea. "I think we could spend weeks here and never run out of things to see."

Brigid nodded. "I think so, too." They continued to point out all the little details around them and finally they took a selfie of the two of them with the river as a backdrop. Holly had made Brigid promise to take lots of photos, so she could see everything when they were all back home again. The thought of the young girl made Brigid wish she were with them to enjoy it all.

"Do you think Holly's having an okay time in Missouri?" Brigid asked as their food arrived. Linc had chosen a steak with a mushroom wine sauce and a twice baked potato as a side. Brigid had decided on what the menu touted as a gourmet beef stew.

"I'm sure she is. That girl knows how to make the best out of even the worst situations. I don't think you have anything to worry about. She knew how to take care of herself long before she met us. I'm sure she's having a wonderful time," Linc said as he cut into his steak.

"I hope so. I'm probably worrying too much, but this was her first time flying and she had to do it all by herself. Then when she got there, she was getting picked up by people she didn't even know," Brigid explained. "That's being pretty brave." She hoped it was just her own nervousness that she was projecting onto Holly.

"Yeah, but she'd spoken to her aunt on the phone a couple times, so it's not as if she's a total stranger. Besides, she has her phone. If anything was really wrong, she'd let you know," he pointed out.

"That's true," Brigid said as she began to dig into her dinner, feeling the tension slip from her shoulders. She took a deep breath and said, "You're probably right, and I'm worrying over nothing."

"At least you care enough to worry. Don't be so hard on yourself," Linc said with a reassuring smile.

"Sometimes I wonder how she feels about living with me. I know she likes it, don't get me wrong, but I wonder if she feels out of place since we aren't legally family or anything like that." Brigid had been thinking about it ever since she and Linc had taken Holly to the airport. Did Holly feel as though she didn't have a family?

"I can see your point. Like maybe she'd be more comfortable if everything were legalized?" he asked.

"Yeah, something like that," Brigid nodded.

"Is that something you want to do? Adopt her legally?" Linc asked. "I have no problem with it, but I just don't want you rushing into anything without thinking thoroughly through it. There's a lot you'd have to do to legally adopt her."

Brigid paused and considered it. It wasn't as if she didn't already think of Holly like a daughter. She constantly worried about her and whether or not she was happy and healthy. But did Holly want to leave things as they were? It was tough to say. "Maybe I should think about it a little more," she finally said. "It's not that I don't want to, it's just that I'm not totally sure it's something she'd feel comfortable with."

"I think that's a good idea," Linc said with a small smile. "Sit with the idea and see how it feels. Maybe we should talk to her about it when we get back home. To another subject. The sauce on the steak and the potatoes are some of the best things I've ever eaten. How's your beef stew?"

"It's the best I've ever had. It has this kind of a gravy that's simply delicious. I'm glad we picked this restaurant."

The waiter walked over to their table and handed each of them a dessert menu. "I hope you left a little room for dessert. People tell me that ours are the best they've ever had."

Linc and Brigid looked at the menu for a moment, then Brigid said, "Well, you're the expert, not us. What would you recommend?"

"My two favorites are the shortbread cookies with dulce de leche filling and the panna cotta with fruit on top."

"We'll take your advice," Linc said. "One of each. We'll split them and see which one is our favorite."

When the waiter brought their desserts, they each tried half of one and half of the other. "Thoughts, Mrs. Olsen?" Linc said.

"Phenomenal. Those were the perfect ending to a perfect meal, but I think we need to walk dinner off. Agree?"

"Yes, both on the quality of the meal and the walk."

They paid the bill and began to stroll along the river to where the boats were loading. After a quick exchange, they purchased two tickets to ride a boat and climbed on board.

"Do you think it's strange for me to be a little excited?" Linc whispered to Brigid after they sat down in their seats.

She smiled. "Really? I don't think it's strange, but I'm a bit surprised. This isn't exactly like skiing or snowboarding. You tend to be more of a thrill seeker and, hopefully, this won't be one of those kinds of rides," she said as she held up her two crossed fingers.

Linc laughed. "I doubt it will be. No, it's just a little different, that's all. I don't think I've ever done anything like this before."

"I really haven't either. Unless you count those round tube rides at the amusement park," Brigid said with a laugh.

By then, the sun had almost completely set and the lights of the city had turned on. A few businesses had strings of lights on them that made everything seem just that much more magical. Listening to the tour guide, they took in the sights and learned a bit about the history of San Antonio as they slowly cruised down the river. Brigid snuggled under Linc's arm, searching for a bit of warmth now that the heat of the day had gone and the evening was cool on the water.

After the tour was over, Linc took Brigid's hand and kissed it. "Do you want to head back, or do you want to walk a little more?"

"I'd like to walk a little more," Brigid said. "I don't feel quite ready to head back yet."

As they were strolling, they heard the sound of music coming from nearby. "I wonder what that is," Linc said. "It almost sounds like a concert."

Ahead of them they saw a group of people outside a bar with flashing lights. "Looks like it might be coming from in there," Brigid pointed out.

When they got closer, it was obvious she was right. Inside a band was playing an upbeat song while couples danced and a few sang along with the band.

"Want to head inside? We can grab a drink and dance for a little while. What do you say?" Linc urged.

Brigid thought about saying no, since everyone inside seemed quite a bit younger than they were. But once she saw the reflection of the sparkling lights in Linc's eyes, she could tell he wanted to.

"Sure," she said. "I haven't danced in a bar in so long I can't even remember the last time."

"No time like the present then," Linc said with a smile. He took her hand and led her inside. They found a seat at the worn wooden bar and ordered drinks. Although Brigid had been apprehensive at first, she found herself enjoying the energy of the upscale bar. It made her feel a bit more vibrant than she was used to, but that was a good thing.

A slow song came on and Linc tossed back the rest of his drink. "Excuse me, beautiful lady?" he began. "May I have this dance?"

Brigid couldn't help but grin, warmed by the alcohol in her system. "Why of course, sir," she said as she took his hand.

He led her to the dance floor where the lights had dimmed to a soft blue. She wrapped her arms around his neck as he pulled her close, and they began to sway with the music. Brigid hadn't ever heard the song before, but it seemed fitting for Linc and her. It was about second chances and finding love after searching for a long time. It was haunting and beautiful, making the moment just that much more magical.

Once it was over, Linc took her by the hand and led her back outside. "I think I'm ready to take my bride back to our honeymoon suite," he said as he kissed her gently.

"Then by all means, let's go," she said with a smile. "I'm ready if you are." Hand in hand, they walked back along the River Walk and headed towards where they'd parked their car. Brigid wasn't sure if it was the drink, the dance, or just the wonderful time she was having, but she felt as if she was floating on air.

CHAPTER FOUR

Larry Barelli was getting tired of being the muscle. It seemed like everywhere he went, that's what was expected of him. When he'd started working as a bartender at El Lobo, he thought he was finally getting away from all of that. Maybe people could tell he was ex-military, but he felt as though people automatically assumed he was a tough guy. He wasn't quite sure what it was that seemed to make him the prime candidate for being the big tough guy that people sometimes needed for a little help.

As far as he was concerned, he was just your average guy. Average height, maybe a slightly bigger build than most, but that was just because he did his best to stay in shape. It was more from a habit he'd gotten into while he was in the army than anything. It wasn't as if he was downing protein shakes and talking about his workouts to anyone who would listen. He just liked to take care of himself and eat things that were healthy.

He was behind the bar once again tonight, hoping that with enough tips, he just might be able to pay his utility bill. He'd been doing fairly well through the winter, but now that the weather had started getting hot, his electric bill had started to climb. It was hard making ends meet, and this job was the only thing he'd been able to land. But it wasn't cutting it.

Larry was in dire need of more money. Not to mention the fact that he still needed to take a trip to visit his mom. She'd fallen a couple of weeks earlier and hurt herself. Even though his sisters had been there to watch over her, he still felt as though he needed to make a trip to see her, but his old truck was a real gas guzzler.

He'd been approached by a guy a few weeks ago about doing some under-the-table work for him. The guy insisted that his name was Bob, but Larry knew when someone was lying to him. The guy's name definitely wasn't Bob, but who was he to argue? When the guy offered him cash to do a little intimidation work for him, Larry gladly accepted. Why not? Everyone seemed to think he was some tough guy. Might as well get paid for it. It wasn't something he planned on doing for long, but he really needed the cash.

So far there had only been a couple of jobs, but it didn't take much for Larry to put two and two together. "Bob" ran an illegal gambling operation, and he needed Larry to convince people to pay up what they owed him. All Larry had to do was show up on the deadbeats' doorstep and they'd been more than eager to hand over the money they owed. Larry had gotten a percentage which helped him catch up on a few of his outstanding bills. Now he really needed to do another job for Bob, so he'd have the funds to take the trip to see his mother.

"Hey handsome, can I get another one?" a petite blonde asked, leaning over the bar, and giving him a look at her ample bosom as she did so. Her perfect white teeth seemed to glow in the blacklight.

"Sure thing," he said with a wink. Girls seemed to fall for his blue eyes and dark hair, which tended to make the tips a little larger towards the end of the night. Nobody tipped quite as well as a drunk girl who wanted in your pants. It probably helped that the bar was in what was considered the tourist district. Something about being on vacation seemed to make some women throw all their inhibitions out the window. Not that he cared as long as it helped his wallet. He poured the woman another drink and slid it across the bar.

"What are you doing later tonight?" she asked seductively.

"I close, so I'm not getting off until after two," he said as he wiped off the bar with a towel.

"Hmm, so when can we get together?" she asked with a sly smile.

She was a direct one which always seemed to make things easier. "I don't know. It's fairly busy right now, but if you stick around, I might have some free time," he said, his voice getting low. He didn't mind a casual hookup once in a while, if the woman was good looking enough.

"Maybe I will," she said before slipping back into the crowd. It was hard telling if he'd actually see her later. Sometimes they'd come on strong and then change their mind when things got right down to it. Not that it really mattered to Larry one way or another. For every one that stood him up, three more were soon in the offering.

His cell phone buzzed in his pocket, pulling him back to reality. He took it out of his pocket and saw that he had a text message from "Bob." He wasn't sure if he should be disappointed or happy. The money was good, but he was starting to feel a little dirty about the whole thing. Something about using intimidation to earn money didn't feel right. Plus, what if things escalated? Eventually, someone wouldn't be so easily swayed. What would Bob expect him to do then?

I have another job for you. Give me a call when you can.

Larry was hopeful that this next person owed a lot and would easily cough it up. Then maybe he'd have enough money to pay off his bills and take the trip to see his mom. After that he could tell Bob he didn't want to do any more work for him. It was a long shot, but he was crossing his fingers that it would work out.

"Hey, Jo?" he said as he got the other bartender's attention. She turned to listen to him as she mixed a drink. She was doing a little dance behind the bar to the beat of the music.

"What's up?" she asked, her nose ring glittering in the lights.

"I have to make a call. Think you can manage on your own for a few minutes?" he asked.

She looked around and nodded. "Sure. Just make it quick," she said as she passed the drink she'd been mixing across the bar.

"Will do," he said as he slipped out from behind the bar and headed towards the rear of the bar. It was much quieter back there and it would be easier to hear Bob. Out on the floor it was almost always impossible to take a call. Too many voices combined with loud music. He punched in the number, put the phone to his ear, and waited.

"Larry, thanks for getting back to me so quickly," he heard on the other end of the line. Bob's gravelly voice sounded as though he'd been smoking for a long time.

"I don't have a whole lot of time," he said. "I'm at work. But I wanted to get back to you before it was late."

"I appreciate that," Bob said. "Do you remember a guy named Mark that you had a little talk with not too long ago?"

"The guy that works at the Alamo?" he asked.

"That's the one. He's still dodging me. I think he's going to need a bit more persuasion."

"Not a problem. You have his home address this time? I remember you were working on it." Larry asked.

"Yes, I do. I'll send it over when we hang up. Obviously, the same rules apply. I don't need anything too serious yet. Just give him a good scare, but make sure when it's all said and done, he knows why you're there. Tell him if he doesn't do what needs to be done, things are going to get worse," Bob instructed. "A lot worse. He owes me a sizeable amount, and I want to start getting back what I'm owed."

Larry nodded and then, realizing that Bob couldn't see him, said,

"Sure. Not a problem."

"You may need to visit the guy at work again. Guy's not home often. He's slippery, but not all that bright. You shouldn't have too much trouble with him. I'm going to have my guys keep trying to dig up some information on him, just in case. I'll check back with you in a few days if I haven't heard anything from you," Bob said.

"Sounds good. Thanks," Larry said before ending the call. Moments later his cell phone buzzed with a text from Bob containing Mark's home address. He looked at the name and address he'd written on a napkin. Mark didn't exactly live in the richest neighborhood in town. Poor guy was probably just down on his luck, but now it was up to Larry to convince him to pay up. Hopefully the guy owed a lot, that way Larry's take from the percentage would be bigger than it had been before. That's the way Bob worked. The more you could get paid off for Bob, the more he'd have to pay you.

Larry figured he'd check out Mark's place first. See if he could catch him coming or going. Maybe he could sneak up on him and surprise the guy. Let him know he's being watched. That would have to be a huge incentive to make someone pay off their gambling debts. After all, who wouldn't want to take care of what they owed if they thought someone was sitting outside their house watching them and just might want to hurt them.

Plan B would be to show up at Mark's workplace, this time while he was working. It wasn't a prospect that Larry really looked forward to, but if it got the job done, so be it. Last time he'd found out when Mark would be getting off work and had waited outside. He'd tried talking to him man to man without being too intimidating. Bob hadn't been too concerned about the urgency of getting his money, so a sort of soft approach had worked. Now it looked like things had changed.

He folded the napkin with Mark's address on it and tucked it in his jeans pocket. He'd find out exactly where the place was tomorrow morning. Then, depending on where Mark lived, he'd plan accordingly. There was no way Larry was going to pass up this opportunity to make some extra cash. He needed to put the fear of God in this Mark guy and get him to pay up and pay up fast. That way he'd get his percentage cut from Bob sooner rather than later.

Even if it meant he had to use a little more of a threat than just his presence to do it. He considered the possibility of using the pistol he kept in his nightstand for added emphasis. It was a little extreme, but it might be necessary in order to speed things up.

Heading back out to the main bar area he wondered if taking his gun would help or make things worse. On one hand, a gun showed you were serious. On the other hand, Bob had specifically instructed him to not get too crazy, otherwise the cops could get involved, and that was bad for business. A couple sitting at the bar waved to get his attention, and he decided he'd worry about Mark later, when he was off work. Then he'd decide how he should handle him.

When he approached the couple, he flashed them his most winning smile and leaned across the bar. "Hey, how's it going? What can I get for you two tonight?" He still had a long night ahead of him. He couldn't afford to be distracted. He pushed Mark, the gun, and his job as an enforcer to the back of his mind and focused on taking the couple's drink order.

CHAPTER FIVE

Brigid woke up the next morning wrapped in Linc's arms. The sun was filtering through the sheers behind the deep red curtains, giving the room a soft, yet ethereal, glow. She smiled as his arm pulled her closer when he felt her stir. She smelled a faint trace of his cologne on his skin, and she breathed it in. The scent still made her feel a slight flutter in her stomach.

"Good morning, Mrs. Olson," he mumbled into her hair. He kissed the back of her head and groaned in contentment. "How'd you sleep?"

"Like a baby," Brigid sighed as she snuggled down deeper into his embrace. "I swear, normally I can never sleep when I'm not in my own bed, but this one is different. I think we need an annulment, because I want to marry this bed instead," she teased.

"Nope, it can't have you. I've already staked my claim," Linc said playfully. "But if you did, I'd like to see you try to get it on the airplane to take it home. That could be entertaining."

"Then I guess I'll just have to enjoy the time I have left with it," she said as she turned around to face him. "Although I have to say, I'm more than a little heartbroken." She pressed her lips to his. "What's on the agenda for the day?"

"I don't know. We can do a little shopping. We definitely need to get souvenirs for everyone," Linc suggested. "Maybe we should go ahead and get that out of the way before we forget?"

"I like that idea. Tomorrow I think I'd like to head to the beach. I'm looking forward to sitting on the sand with an ocean view," she said. "I want to feel the sea spray on my skin. It feels like it's been forever since I felt the sand between my toes."

"We can head that way today if you'd prefer," Linc said as he propped himself up on his arm. He began to brush back her hair with his fingers. "It's not a big deal. Shopping can wait for another day."

"No, I watched the weatherman for a couple of minutes before we went to bed last night, and there's a chance for rain this afternoon. Tomorrow's supposed to be clear all day. I like your idea. We can wing it like we did at the River Walk yesterday. I don't know when I've had such a wonderful lazy evening. It's going to be hard to top that."

"Well, we'll have to see what we can do about that. Maybe we should hide from the world and stay in bed all day," he suggested as he began to kiss her neck. "I can think of a few things we could do to entertain ourselves."

Brigid giggled. "I don't know if you'd have the energy. Heck, I'm not sure I would!"

Linc smiled before inhaling deeply. He lifted his nose and said, "Do you smell that?"

"Smell what?" Brigid asked. She inhaled deeply but couldn't smell anything out of the ordinary. Only the smell of her husband and the comfortable sheets they were cuddled beneath, which smelled a little like roses.

"I think I smell food cooking," Linc said. "I wonder if John's making breakfast. It smells amazing." As he finished his sentence, his stomach grumbled loudly.

"Sounds like your stomach agrees. Come on, let's get dressed and go downstairs," Brigid suggested.

She threw back the blankets and climbed out of the bed. The area rug covering the dark wood floor felt soft under her bare feet. She reached for the clothes she'd laid out for the day and began to get dressed.

"I may have to find out his recipe. Whatever that is, it smells heavenly," Linc commented as he pulled on his shirt.

"I'm trying to figure out why your stomach is growling so loud after that big dinner we had last night," Brigid marveled. "Are we going to go bankrupt trying to keep you fed?"

"Hey, I'm an active guy with a healthy appetite. Don't blame me," he said as he held his hands up in a sign of mock surrender. "Besides, I'm telling you it really smells good."

They put on their shoes and Brigid quickly ran a brush through her hair before they stepped out into the hall.

"You're right," Brigid said, turning to Linc. "It does smell amazing." As they descended the stairs, they gave their tell-tale creak, letting John and Charlie know that someone was coming down the stairs. When they got to the bottom of the stairs Charlie came trotting into the main room, his tongue hanging out and tail wagging.

"Hey there boy," Brigid said as she bent down to greet him. "How are you this morning?"

John emerged through the kitchen's swinging door with a bright smile. "Well good morning! Would you care for some breakfast? I was just making something for Charlie and me. I can make some for you too, if you'd like to join us." He looked happy to see them, his hair still a wild mop on top of his head.

"That would be great, if you don't mind," Linc said happily. "Whatever you're making, it smells phenomenal. It's actually what got me out of bed this morning."

John signaled for them to follow him as he turned back through the door. "I'm making southwest omelets. You can sit at the counter while I whip up a couple more."

"I don't think I've ever had one of those before," Brigid said as she looked at the ingredients on the counter. "What's in it?"

"It's an omelet filled with chili and cheese," the older man said as he returned to the stove. Brigid looked around the spacious kitchen with envy. It was big enough to have a breakfast counter along one side with an island in the middle. There were cabinets everywhere, and they were all painted a bright white which made the kitchen look as if it was brand new. How he managed to keep them so clean and gleaming was a mystery to her. She was fairly sure if she tried to have white cabinets in her kitchen at home, they'd never be clean.

"Chili for breakfast?" Linc said surprised. "I've never heard of anything like that."

"Neither had I," John admitted. "But one time my wife and I stopped for the night in Gallup, New Mexico, while we were on a road trip. The next morning we went into a little diner that was attached to the hotel, and I saw it on the menu. I love chili, and I love breakfast, so I was eager to give it a try. I've been hooked ever since. If you don't like chili, I can put something else in yours," he began.

"No, that's fine," Brigid said as she turned to Linc who was nodding affirmatively. "It sounds odd, but we're more than willing to give it a try."

"Excellent!" John said with a wide smile. "The chili is my family recipe, so you won't find anything like it in any restaurant," he said proudly.

"Then I definitely want to give it a shot," Linc said. "I love trying new things and secret family recipes are always delicious. I don't think I've come across one yet that didn't make me wish I was a part of the family."

"My kind of man," John said as he began cooking their omelets. "I used to be the same way, but anymore food doesn't like me as much as I like it. I always make an exception for chili, though. It's my one weakness. If you put chili on it, I'll probably eat it," he said with a hearty laugh.

Soon the omelets were done, and he set the plates in front of Linc and Brigid. The chili was oozing out from the omelets and there was plenty of cheese melting on top and inside. He'd garnished them with chopped green onions. The smell coming from the plates had their mouths watering.

"I like to put a little sour cream on mine," John said as he pulled out a bowl and sat it before them. "Help yourself if you're so inclined."

Both Brigid and Linc took a spoonful of the sour cream and topped their omelets with it before finally digging in. Brigid wasn't sure what to expect when she took her first bite, but she was pleasantly surprised. The flavors of the omelet, along with the robust chili, was a pairing she never would have thought of.

"Is that clove I taste in the chili?" Linc asked after a few bites.

"Sure is," John said approvingly as he joined them. "You must be a cook yourself."

"I am," Linc admitted. "Although I specialize more in Italian dishes than anything else."

Brigid nodded. "He even makes his own pasta on occasion," she bragged. "But this is really good. I'm going to have to make something like this for Holly when we get back home," she said turning to Linc who nodded in agreement.

"Is Holly your daughter?" John asked.

Brigid thought about explaining everything, but decided not to for the sake of time. "Yes. She's visiting family in Missouri while we're on our honeymoon."

"That's great," he said. "My kids are grown and have moved away. They come and visit occasionally, but usually it's just me and Charlie here." He looked down at the dog who was staring at him expectantly. "You're just going to have to wait, boy. I have things to do." He said as he leaned back and began to eat.

"Does he want to go for a walk?" Brigid asked.

"Yeah, he likes to take a trip around the block every morning, but I have a few things I need to get done first before we can go," John admitted.

"We could take him for you, if you don't mind," Linc offered.

"I'm sure you have plenty of things you want to do while you're on your honeymoon. We don't want to interfere with what you had planned for the day," John said.

"It's no trouble at all," Brigid interjected. "I kind of miss taking my dog for his morning walk, so taking Charlie would make me feel good.

John chuckled. "If you don't mind, you won't hear me complain. I was always taught that if someone offers you help, you're a fool if you don't accept."

Once they'd finished their breakfast and thoroughly thanked John for it, Brigid got Charlie's leash and clipped it on his collar. They promised John they'd take good care of Charlie before they left the kitchen, leaving John to clean up. She and Linc led the dog outside and onto the sidewalk.

Large puffy clouds were moving in, giving them some intermittent shade. A slight breeze ruffled Brigid's hair and made her close her eyes for a moment, soaking it all in. It was a beautiful morning, and she was glad Charlie had wanted to take a little walk. Brigid and Linc strolled in companionable silence, allowing Charlie to guide them on their route.

"He seems to know this route by heart," Brigid said as Charlie automatically turned the corner and continued around the block.

"Well, who knows how many times he's walked this way," Linc said. "You can tell he's much older than Jett. He probably knows every smell and sight along the way, too."

Linc and Brigid simply enjoyed the morning and their short bit of exercise before returning to the B & B. By the time they got back, Charlie and Brigid had become fast friends. It wasn't that he rejected Linc, he just seemed to prefer Brigid. At times he'd stop and encourage her to pet him. When they entered the B & B and she unhooked his leash, he stayed by her side like a faithful friend.

"Okay, Charlie. I've got other things to do now, but maybe we can go for a walk again soon," she told her new four-legged friend. He gave her hand a lick before trotting off to find John.

CHAPTER SIX

Zoey Hill hadn't been working in the gift shop at the Alamo for very long. She was taking a little time off before she started college. She was completely over writing essays, taking exams, studying, and generally doing things she didn't want to do. Besides, she was making decent enough money for now, and she had an opportunity to meet people from all over the world, so in her book it was a bit of a win-win situation. She and her roommate were able to make ends meet, so there really wasn't much to complain about.

When Zoey had met Mark, a fellow employee at the Alamo, she couldn't believe that an older man could be interested in her. He seemed like such a nice guy, sweet, attentive, and kind. They'd spent a little time together outside of work, but for the most part they snuck in a few private moments throughout the day while they were at work. It was nice having someone she looked forward to seeing every day. It definitely made it easier to get up and come to work on those days she'd rather stay in bed.

"Hey, beautiful," Mark said as he came up behind her. She was sitting at one of the tables in the small break room munching on a bag of potato chips she'd gotten from the vending machine.

"Hey, yourself," she said with a smile. "What are you doing?" He circled around her, pulled out a chair, and sat beside her.

"Coming to spend some time with you," he said with a sly smile. "I just finished with a tour and thought I'd go to the gift shop and see you, but you weren't there."

"No, I had to open this morning, so I came in early," she explained. "That means my breaks are a little earlier today."

Mark nodded. "I see. What are you doing tonight?" he asked as he leaned over and gave her a kiss on the neck.

"I have a couple of friends coming over for a movie night," she said with a smile. "What are you doing?"

"Not sure. I was going to see if you wanted to do something but I didn't realize you had plans," he stuck his lip out as if he were pouting and Zoey couldn't help but feel bad.

"I'm sorry. Can I take a raincheck? I've had this planned for over a week, and it's a little too late to back out now." She really liked Mark and didn't want to give him the impression she wasn't interested.

"Sure, that's not a problem," he said easily. "Anything for you." He gently tapped her on the end of her nose, making her blush.

"I heard Miguel is retiring soon. Do you think Celine will choose you as the lead tour guide?" Zoey asked.

"Sure would be nice," Mark admitted. "I could really use the pay increase."

She nodded. "I think we all could. They aren't exactly paying us top dollar here, although I've had worse. Don't ever work in retail, especially in the mall."

Mark turned his focus intently on Zoey. "Have you heard anything about when she'll make a decision?"

Zoey felt herself shrink under his intense scrutiny. "No. Why would I? I barely even talk to the woman. She's your boss, not mine."

Mark nodded. "Right, right. I forget sometimes. Well, if you hear anything, will you let me know?"

"Sure, but you'd probably hear something before I would," she said distractedly. She pulled her phone out of her pocket so she could text her roommate. There was something she was supposed to get at the store after work, but she couldn't remember what it was.

Mark started to stand up from his chair, and then paused. "Why would I hear first?" he asked carefully.

Zoey thought Mark was acting strangely. He'd never seemed so scattered and all over the place before. The way he was looking at her was starting to make her think something unusual was going on with him. Normally he was very calm and collected. Now, he almost seemed angry about something.

"I don't know. Maybe because you're in the same department? It seems like us gift shop people always hear things last," she said as she frowned at him. *What is going on?* she thought. *Something has to be up.*

"Yeah, I suppose that's true," he said with a chuckle. "Well, still, let me know what you hear." After he stood up, he ran his hand along Zoey's back. "Maybe we can do something together this weekend," he said hopefully. Whatever he'd been irritated about seemed to be gone. Zoey was starting to wonder if he had some sort of drug problem since his words and actions seemed to be somewhat erratic.

She nodded. "Sure. That sounds great." She gave him a reassuring smile that didn't seem to make it all the way to her eyes. Something was off with Mark, and she was determined to find out what it was. When he left the break room, she saw through the window in the door that he didn't turn towards the right like he usually did. Instead, he turned left, which led toward the other offices.

Her brain told her he was probably just going to see if anyone else had heard much about Miguel and his retirement, but something, call it idle curiosity, made her follow him. She slipped out of the break room, gently closing the door behind her.

Catching sight of him turning the corner, she quietly walked down the hall after him and peeked around the corner. He headed through the halls, turning to look over his shoulder from time to time, but she was out of sight. It looked as though he was making sure he wasn't being followed, which was all the more reason for her to keep tailing him. She wanted to know what he was up to. Maybe it would give her an idea as to why he'd been acting so strange when they were talking.

Although it was still early in their relationship, if he had a problem, she wanted to see if there was something she could do to help. It was just part of her nature. She didn't like to see anyone in trouble or upset, and if she did, she always wanted to try and help.

A few moments later she heard him talking to someone near the end of the "Employees Only" section of the building. It was darker down there, but while he was distracted, she slipped into a little alcove with a water fountain and some potted plants. It wasn't a very big space, but neither was she. Hiding behind a large plant, she had a better view of what he was doing.

Whoever he was talking to was just out of her eyesight. Mark was speaking in a low tone to the person, too low for Zoey to make out what he was saying. The light from Celine's nearby office window helped Zoey see one side of his face. He reached out and pulled the person towards him from where they'd been standing just around the corner. Even in the dim light, Zoey knew who it was.

When she watched Mark place his hands on either side of Celine's face, she wondered if something was wrong. Maybe the older woman was crying and she'd been hiding, not wanting anyone to see her? Rumor had it that her marriage was on the rocks. Perhaps she'd hidden away from everyone to have a moment by herself, and Mark happened upon her.

Suddenly, Celine reached out and pulled Mark to her. Her mouth landed on his and Zoey half expected to see him pull away. Only, he didn't. Instead he deepened the kiss and pressed himself against her. A janitor whistled at the other end of the hall as he walked by and they quickly pulled apart. Both of them looked nervous and seemed to be afraid that the janitor might have seen them.

After hearing his whistle fade as he continued by, Celine pulled Mark into her office and shut the door. The door was all wood, but there was a large window just to the left of it. The blinds were still open, but Mark and Celine were out of sight.

Just as she was thinking about giving up, Zoey saw Celine through the window. She'd perched herself on the edge of her desk and hiked up her skirt and spread her legs. Zoey had a clear view of her. Her jaw dropped when she realized Celine wasn't wearing any underwear.

Mark moved towards her and began passionately embracing her. Zoey pulled out her phone and began video recording them. This was the age of technology and now she had proof that he had lied to her.

Zoey was horrified, but she couldn't bring herself to look away. She made herself watch, so the next time Mark told her he wanted to spend time with her, she'd remember what she was seeing. Her heart broke into a million pieces as she watched Mark make love to his boss.

Finally, Mark turned around and without seeing her, closed the blinds, completely blocking her view, but she'd seen and recorded enough. Zoey wasn't sure if she could have handled watching any more. She stopped the recording, closed her phone and slid it back into her pocket.

Zoey couldn't believe it. Mark was having an affair with Celine, too. Could there be others? Her mind began to race as she thought of all the other women working at the Alamo. Had he been doing it for fun? Leading her along, letting her think that she actually meant something to him?

From the way he and Celine had carried on, it was fairly obvious this wasn't the first time they'd done something like this. Mentally running through the list of other women who worked there, her heart began to sink. Who said his betrayal was limited just to the women who worked there? He could be stringing along women from all over San Antonio.

How many times had Mark pulled Zoey into a dark corner or closet only to ravish her? Her stomach churned as she thought about the possibility of being with Mark after he'd been with Celine and lord knows who else. Now she was wondering if she should get tested for the presence of any sexually transmitted diseases. The idea enraged her that he could be so careless. Did he have no decency?

Stepping out from behind the potted plant where she'd been hiding, Zoey felt as though she was walking through a fog. How could he do this to her? How could he take her heart and stomp all over it as if it was nothing? Did he think she was just some dumb kid that didn't deserve any respect? Maybe she needed to teach him a lesson.

After all, she was far from stupid. She'd been one of the brightest kids in her class. Just because she hadn't chosen to go to college right after she'd finished high school didn't mean she wasn't intelligent. Perhaps she needed to show him exactly who he was messing with.

As Zoey headed back to the gift shop, the thought of scaring Mark into submission pleased her. She'd ask him to meet her and tell him she knew all about Celine and was planning on telling everyone. She had a video as proof, and once people saw it, he and Celine would be looking for new jobs.

She'd tell him she was planning on posting the video online for the world to see. A few good hashtags and it would spread like wildfire, completely ruining Mark and Celine's reputation. But first, she had to show Mark who was boss before tearing his world to shreds.

Zoey began to smile as she headed back to the gift shop. There was no way she'd let Mark get away with this. She'd make him suffer. It would be the last time anyone would double cross her. A cold yet calm rage was running through her veins. When she was finished with him, Mark would never want to cross her again.

CHAPTER SEVEN

With the top down on the rental car and the sun shining, Brigid and Linc were headed to Corpus Christi for their day at the beach. It was one part of the trip that Brigid had especially looked forward to. When she'd lived in California, she'd loved sitting by the ocean and just lounging the day away. Watching the Pacific Ocean tide roll in had always seemed to put things into perspective for her.

Whenever she'd felt life was too overwhelming, like with her ex-husband, work, or anything else, that's where she'd go to relax. Towards the end of her marriage it seemed like she spent more time there than she did at home. Brigid took a deep breath to clear away those old thoughts and feelings, bringing herself back to the present.

Yesterday they'd bought gifts for everyone back home and now they were cruising with the top down towards a day at the beach. Brigid felt like she was a small child on her way to somewhere fantastic. She might even take a dip in the warm waters of the Gulf of Mexico at some point, but just feeling her toes in the sand and listening to the sound of the surf was more than enough for her.

"I can't tell you how much I'm looking forward to this," Brigid said as she felt the warmth of the sun shining down on her.

"Me too," Linc said with a broad smile. "The sun is shining, and the waves are calling me. My adventurous side is ready to try something new."

"Let me guess. You plan on surfing," Brigid said as she looked over at him.

"Don't you want to give it a shot?" he asked as he glanced at her with mild curiosity.

"Not really," Brigid admitted. "Seems like it would take way too much effort. I'm more in the mood for things that are relaxing, not something that will stress me out."

"Party pooper," Linc said playfully. He winked when she gave him a mock serious glare.

"By all means, try your surfing. I'll be the one cheering you on from the beach," she said breaking into a smile.

"Deal," Linc said. "While you're on the beach relaxing, why don't you look online and see if there's anything else you want to do while we're in this area? We have all day. Might as well take in any other sights you may be interested in," he said as they began to cross the bridge that took them to Padre Island. The scent of the ocean was intoxicating and Brigid took a deep breath.

"Good idea," Brigid said. "I'll bet there are plenty of interesting things we could check out after we get a little sun. I'm sure they have something around here besides a beautiful beach."

It wasn't long before they arrived at the beach and began to unload a few things from the car. Linc helped her stake out a nice spot in the sand even though he was more than ready to hit the waves. When she was situated, he jogged off towards a nearby beach shack that offered surfing lessons. The way he hustled over to it reminded Brigid of a little kid getting in line to see Santa Claus. She smiled to herself as she took off her wrap and got comfortable.

Brigid had set up her chair and umbrella close enough to the water so she'd be able to see Linc's surfing lesson. She smiled as she watched him carrying the surfboard. He looked like a natural, even though he'd told her he had yet to learn how. Brigid wondered how she'd been so lucky to have such a wonderful man like Linc become her husband. He was so adventurous, yet he never pushed her to do something she didn't want to do, which was huge for her.

Her first husband was always insisting that they do the things he wanted to do, without any concern for what she might want to do. Linc simply accepted her for who she was, which was one of those people who was perfectly happy watching others have fun. She didn't need to go out and try to balance on a surfboard and attempt to ride a few waves. Her world was much more laid back and relaxed which was a stark difference from Linc's passion to try almost everything once.

As she watched him paddle out in the water with his instructor, she began to think about Holly. She wondered if everything was really going as well with her as she'd said in her message to Brigid earlier that morning. Brigid hadn't been able to help it and had finally sent her a text inquiring as to how she was doing on her trip to Springfield, Missouri to visit her aunt and her family. Naturally, Holly had insisted everything was fine, and that she was having a good time.

That had made Brigid feel better, but she still worried about the young girl. She knew even if Holly wasn't having a good time, there was no way she'd come right out and say so. *Of course that also didn't mean she wasn't having a good time,* Brigid reminded herself. *She could just as easily be having a great time.*

But for some reason, Holly's assurance hadn't made her feel any better. She began to worry that Holly would return from Missouri with a different outlook on Cottonwood Springs and her life with Brigid. Maybe she'd really hit it off with her aunt, uncle, and cousins and decide that she'd been too hasty in wanting to stay in Cottonwood Springs. What if she decided she wanted to move to Springfield? Brigid didn't have the authority to tell her she couldn't. After all, it was Holly's family who lived in Springfield, and she could move there to live with them if she chose to do so.

Brigid shook her head to clear away her negative thoughts. "There you go, overthinking again," she whispered to herself. She reached for her bag and pulled out a paperback she'd brought along. Since she edited books for a living, it wasn't very often she felt like reading something in her ever-growing stack of books that she wanted to read. Usually after buying the books, they'd just sit on a shelf, collecting dust.

She'd viewed this vacation as an opportunity to at least start a book that she really wanted to read. She scanned the ocean for a glimpse of Linc before opening the book and picking up where she'd left off on the plane. She decided to read for a bit before she got her phone out and began looking for other things to do while they were in the area. After all, they had nothing but time on their hands. Sighing as she slipped further down into her chair, she settled in and reminded herself they were here to relax.

*****

"That was amazing," Linc said, joining Brigid under the umbrella. He was breathing heavily with salt water dripping from his hair. A huge grin was spread across his face.

"It looked like you were really getting the hang of it," she said proudly. Leaning over, she gave him a quick kiss. "Great job."

"I thought so, too. I wish we had a beach near us. I think I could get used to this," he said still beaming. He stretched his legs out and leaned back on the warm sand propped up on one arm.

"I'm sure you do," she said as she tucked her book in her bag. "I did a little searching while you were channeling your inner surfer and found a few things we could check out," she said as she pulled out her phone.

"Let's hear them," he said as he stretched out and closed his eyes.

"There's the USS Lexington," Brigid began. "There's also a surf museum and the seawall downtown which seems to be something people like to check out. I even found out that there's a water garden and the South Texas Walk of Fame."

"Really?" Linc asked surprised. "There's more here than I expected."

"That's only part of it," Brigid said as she pulled a notebook from her bag. "I wrote down a few more. I can't remember all of them."

"Well, we can do whatever you want, babe," he said. "I've surfed, so I've completed my mission for the day. Everything else is just icing on the cake. Especially if I get to do it with you." He smiled at her with that cute boyish grin which had won her heart right from the beginning.

"I think I'd like to visit the Texas State Aquarium which is nearby," she said as she scanned over her list. "There are a few different beaches on the list that we can stop and look at if we want to, but I think checking out the USS Lexington, the water gardens, and the seawall will be fun too. We can take lots of pictures to show everybody back home."

Linc pulled the notebook from her hands and tossed it in her beach bag. "How about we also just drive around and see what jumps out at us. You never know what you might be missing when you're focused on getting from point A to point B." He grinned at her, knowing she loved her lists and being organized. Asking Brigid to do anything on a whim wasn't easy.

Looking thoroughly flustered by him tossing her list, she glanced from the notebook to Linc and then back again. She opened her mouth to object but then caught herself. "Okay," she finally said.

"Okay?" Linc asked, surprised. "Is my beautiful, control freak bride actually going to release the reins just a little?" He was forever trying to get her to relax and do things on a whim, but it went completely against everything she'd ever known. But now she was willing to give his way a shot. After all, what did they have to lose?

"Maybe," she reluctantly relented. "But just a little. I'm pretty set on wanting to see a few things, and I don't want to miss them because we get lost," she said giving him a pointed look.

"Hey, I can get on board with that," he said as he raised his hands in mock surrender. "Just the fact that you're willing to give my way a shot is amazing. I love you, Brigid," he said as he leaned forward and gave her a kiss. He took her hand and began to run his thumb back and forth across it.

"I love you too, Linc," she said smiling. "You know, I'm really not that much of a control freak," she pointed out.

He shrugged. "I know. But I still really like teasing you about it anyway," he admitted.

Brigid laughed. "Whatever makes you happy, I guess. It doesn't bother me one bit."

"Well, are you ready to leave?" he asked. "If we're going to check out all those places on your list, we shouldn't lay around here much longer."

"You're probably right," Brigid admitted. "Let's pack up. If we have any time left after we do everything, we can always return to this beach."

"Anything for you, my love," Linc said as he helped her to her feet. They packed up their belongings and made their way back to the car, walking hand in hand.

"I think we may have to come back here again sometime. Maybe we could bring Holly," Linc suggested as he organized their things in the car's trunk.

Brigid cast a long gaze at the ocean and smiled. "That's a great idea. I bet she'd love it here. Maybe next time we can get a hotel right here on the beach," she suggested.

"I like that idea," he said happily. "Then I can get up early to surf and watch the sun rise at the same time."

Brigid shook her head. "Anything to get to surf a little more, hmm?"

"You got that right," he said with a laugh as they got in the car and he started it up.

CHAPTER EIGHT

Jerry Martinez had been working as a tour guide longer than anyone else at the Alamo. He'd started working there when he'd gotten close to retirement age. His body wasn't exactly what it used to be, making his job at the auto repair shop where he worked almost impossible. Yet when he'd tried to stay at home, he'd felt as if he was going stir crazy.

Since then, he'd put his heart into being a tour guide. He always made sure he was patient with each and every visitor, answering questions to the best of his knowledge or giving them suggestions where to go to find their answers if he didn't know. It was much more interesting than he'd originally thought it would be. San Antonio was rich with history, but he'd never quite realized how interesting that history was. After all, the Alamo wasn't just built for the battle that happened there.

Before he started working at the Alamo, he wasn't aware of how many people visited San Antonio. People from every state in the U.S and even from countries all around the world. It was amazing how diverse their visitors were. Jerry felt as though he probably learned as much from them as they did from him. It was a great way to spend his retirement years. It was almost as if rather than traveling, the travel came to him. For an older man, that was definitely a blessing, plus it was a lot cheaper.

"I heard Miguel is retiring," Shavonne said to him as they stood near the front of the Alamo, waiting for another group of tourists to arrive. She often gravitated to him and helped keep him in the loop about what was going on at their historic place of employment. Many of the younger employees avoided him, but not Shavonne. She loved to listen to his stories and he, in turn, listened to her.

"I heard something about that, too," Jerry admitted. "Someone said Celine has been trying to decide who's going to take his job."

"Well, whoever it is, they need to really know their stuff. Miguel is practically a walking encyclopedia when it comes to the Alamo," Shavonne chuckled. She was quite a bit younger than Jerry, probably in her late twenties, but she was his favorite person to work with. She was a no-nonsense person and did her job well.

"That's very true," Jerry said. Secretly, he'd been hoping he'd get the promotion. It wasn't the reason he'd started learning all the information about the Alamo, but once he realized how much he knew, he felt he definitely was the man for the job.

Shavonne gave him a sideways look. "Think you might get it?"

"I hope so," Jerry said. "The only ones who really seem to know their stuff around here are you and me. The other guides don't seem nearly as dedicated as we are. It would be a shame to see it go to any of them."

"I heard she's going to announce her decision later today or tomorrow. Miguel only has a week left, and she wants to give him a chance to show the new person the ropes. Although, I can't imagine it's too hard of a job." Shavonne said as she crossed her arms in front of her.

"All I know is that it better be you," she said. "If not you, I'm not afraid to hope for myself. If it's anyone else, I'm going to pitch a fit." She set her jaw like she meant it, too. Jerry knew she wasn't afraid to speak up when she didn't feel something was right. He was just glad he was on her good side.

"You don't really think she'd pick someone else, do you?" Jerry asked. "I mean, the others…"

"Yeah, I know. All I'm saying is she better not," Shavonne said as they heard a group of people approaching.

As a tour group entered through the main doors, Jerry said, "You take this one, I'll wait for the next group."

"You sure?" Shavonne asked.

"Sure. I think I'll go talk to Celine and see if she's made a decision yet. I don't know about you, but I'm not a fan of waiting around," Jerry told her. Which was true. He'd gotten fairly impatient when it came to decisions in his older years. There was no beating around the bush with him.

She nodded. "Let me know what you find out," she said before plastering on her trademark bright happy smile and stepping forward to greet the visitors. She began with her typical introduction as he turned to walk away.

Jerry slipped around in back, heading for Celine's office. As he walked towards her office, he thought about exactly what he was going to say to her. There was a part of him that wanted to insist that she appoint him to the soon-to-be-vacant position. After all, no one else was nearly as qualified as he was. That wasn't vanity talking, it was simply the cold hard truth. No one else put in the time and effort needed to learn above and beyond what was expected of them.

Granted, it was sufficient for the average visitor, but there were some people who came wanting to know even more. He'd been teaching Shavonne bits and pieces of what he'd learned, which was why he'd understand if she was given the job. Jerry wasn't blind to the fact that he was past retirement age. But if Celine gave the job to anyone else, he would not be happy. When he was almost to her office, the door opened and she stepped out. Surprised, she took a step back. "Jerry, what can I do for you?"

"I wanted to talk to you about the head tour guide position," he said as he tugged at his sleeves, making sure he looked presentable. It didn't do any good to expect a promotion if you looked disheveled all the time. A fact one or two of the younger men could take to heart.

"Please, come in," Celine said as she gestured for him to join her in her office. He stepped inside and sat down in one of the simple wooden chairs across from her desk as she shut the door. "What about the head tour guide position did you want to talk about?"

"I wanted to make sure that you knew I was extremely interested in that job. I've been rated as one of the most knowledgeable guides here, and I think that should count for something," he began.

"And it does, Jerry. I truly value all the hard work you've put into learning about this place. Your tour groups are always so appreciative of the knowledge you give them," Celine said carefully as she sat down in her chair. "I don't believe we've had a single complaint about you since you started with us. And that's been, what, two or three years now? That's pretty impressive considering some of the visitors we get. Some of them can be quite a handful."

"Which is why I think I deserve Miguel's job," Jerry said. He was sure she could see his point, so why put it off? In his mind, the best course of action was the one that took you where you wanted to be. He'd always been a direct person. That way, the other person knew exactly where he stood. There was no way Celine could turn him down if she knew he wanted the job.

"I appreciate that, Jerry. I really do. But I have someone else in mind for the position," Celine said as she leaned forward on her desk.

That took Jerry by surprise. He hadn't really expected her to pass him over. "Excuse me?" he asked. "Then you must have chosen Shavonne."

Celine shook her head. "I'm afraid not, although she is very good at her job, too. No, I've selected someone else. I may still change my mind, but it's highly doubtful."

"Who?" Jerry asked, doing his best to control his rising temper. He was frustrated and disappointed. Didn't all his hard work count for something?

"Mark," Celine said finally.

"Mark? Why in the devil would you choose him?" Jerry asked as he leaned back and crossed his arms across his chest. He had to reign himself in. This was his boss, after all.

"I strongly considered you, Jerry," she admitted. "But I was concerned about your age. I know you're already past retirement and I didn't want to train you only to have you..."

"Die," Jerry supplied.

Celine smiled politely. "No, I was going to say retire. I'm just not sure how long you'll be sticking around. It was a hard choice, and I almost did choose you. Of course, I haven't said anything to Mark yet. He may not want the position, in which case I may offer it to you." She shrugged her shoulders slightly.

"That kid doesn't have the common sense to think before he opens his mouth, let alone coordinate the tour guides. He'll screw this place up in no time." Jerry was having a hard time choosing his words. What he really wanted to do was let out a string of expletives and hit something, but he had to keep his cool. He had to show Celine he was still the better choice for the job.

"I'm sure there will be a snag or two. There always is when someone starts a new position, but I think he will manage just fine. I hope you will show him the same courtesy you've given Miguel. Oh, and please don't say anything to anyone. I haven't spoken with him yet." She gave him a small but dismissive smile.

Jerry stood up. "Thank you for your time," he said curtly before hurrying out of the office.

He couldn't believe it. Mark? That guy was a few sandwiches short of a picnic and was more than just a little lazy. He didn't give his visitors nearly the experience Jerry did, and he didn't treat the Alamo with the respect it deserved. On more than one occasion, Jerry had seen him leave his trash around or tell a visitor he simply didn't know something. It drove him crazy.

This was a place of reverence, not just any old tourist spot. Treating it with anything other than complete and total respect was a travesty. Of course, it seemed as though anything old and historic wasn't worth a hill of beans anymore. Didn't Celine see that? Didn't she notice all the little things that added up indicating Mark was the wrong guy for the job?

That was when what Celine had said sunk in with him. She said if Mark didn't accept the job, it would be Jerry's. So how do you get a cocky little pipsqueak to turn down a job promotion? He probably wouldn't. Jerry had heard Mark talking about gambling with one of the janitors once. It had sounded like the kid was in debt up to his eyeballs. There was virtually no way someone who needed money would turn down a raise. Not willingly.

But maybe... Jerry began to think. *Maybe I can convince him to quit.* Celine had said that he was passed over because she didn't know how long he would continue to work there. If Jerry could get Mark to quit, that would leave the spot wide open for him to fill. But how could he get him to quit? The guy was slick, so it would probably take something fairly big to motivate him to quit.

Jerry made it back to the main hall, still thinking through a plan. He thought that if he could scare Mark enough, maybe he'd leave. It was a longshot, but pretty much the only thing Jerry had going for him at this point. There was no way he was going to get passed over for this promotion. He'd worked hard to show that he was capable.

The long hours on his feet were starting to get to his knees, but a cushy desk job would be right up his alley. All he had to do was get rid of Mark. But how to do that? Perhaps there was a way to make him feel that this job wasn't all it was cracked up to be. Maybe make him feel unsafe? An idea began to brew in Jerry's mind, and he couldn't help but smile.

CHAPTER NINE

After the long drive back to the Silver Star B & B, Linc and Brigid shuffled in the front door. It had been a full day, but a wonderful one. Their skin was still warm from the sun, and Brigid could feel the salt in her hair. It made her feel twenty years younger.

"How was the beach?" John called out from his spot near the fireplace. Charlie trotted over to greet them as they entered the room, licking their hands and giving them a little bump with his nose.

"Amazing," Brigid said with a smile. "We couldn't have asked for a better day."

"That's great. I'm happy for you. You just never know what might blow in off the ocean. I was afraid an unexpected shower might pop up. That happens every once in a while, about this time of year. Did you get a chance to try your hand at surfing, Linc?" he asked as he folded his paper.

Brigid and Linc joined him by the small fire he'd built. It wasn't cold out, but it gave a cozy feeling to the room.

"I sure did. I think I've been bitten by the surfing bug. I was telling Brigid I wish there was somewhere closer to home where I could practice," he said as they sat down.

John nodded. "I've never been much of a surfer, but I did do a fair bit of sailing in my day," he admitted.

"Really?" Brigid asked. "I bet that was wonderful."

"It was. My wife, Francis, and I would sail out until we couldn't see land anymore and then have a picnic. We'd just forget our troubles while we were out there. It was kind of a thing with us. When we were stressed or worried about something, we'd sail out and say that we left our worries on the shore." The older man looked a little misty-eyed. "Those were the days."

"She must have been a very special woman," Brigid said softly. Her heart broke for the kind old man. She couldn't imagine losing the love of your life and having to continue on without them.

"That she was. I still miss her every day, but I do my best to keep plugging away like I know she'd want me to," he said with a smile. "She was never one for sympathy, that woman. Always wanted everyone to be happy, even at her own expense."

"I'm sure she's smiling down on you. This place looks wonderful. You've done a really nice job of keeping it up," Linc said reassuringly.

"Thanks. She's probably got a few things to say about a couple of my choices, but I think all in all she'd be happy with it." John looked around the room as if he were looking at it from a new perspective.

"If you don't mind me asking, what happened to her?" Brigid asked.

"Cancer, I'm afraid. She'd had a bit of melanoma cut off two years before. The doctors kept checking her over and said everything was clear. But one morning we were sitting on the front porch drinking our coffee, and she started losing her vision. I rushed her to the hospital only to find out she had a large tumor on her brain. It ended up taking her right after she got her first round of chemo." He sighed. "I guess it was just her time," he said.

"I'm so sorry," Brigid said.

He smiled at her faintly. "The B & B hadn't been opened very long. To be honest, I almost sold it. I just didn't want to stay here without her. But one night I had a dream, and she came to me. It was her, but she looked the way she had when we were younger.

"We were out at sea on our boat, her long hair blowing in the breeze. She turned and asked me to keep it going for her. When I woke up the next morning, the dream felt like it had been real. I took it as a sign and did just as she asked me to do. Now that I look back on it, I don't think she steered me wrong."

"That's beautiful," Linc said. He reached over and squeezed Brigid's hand. "You two must have had quite a connection."

"We did," John said nodding. He yawned. "We were like two peas in a pod. But I guess it was her time to go, so I do my best not to question it. Doesn't do me any good, anyway. It's best not to think too much about some things, because it only ends up making things worse. Instead, I try to make the most out of the days I have left and keep plugging away until I can be with her again."

He patted his palm on the arm of the rocking chair. "Well, it's past this old man's bedtime. You two can stay here and enjoy the fire as long as you like. There are a few more logs in the wood rack. I better get some rest if I'm going to be weeding the flower beds tomorrow. I'm not as young as I pretend to be, so I tend to need lots of beauty rest. You two have a good night," he said as he stood.

"You too," Linc and Brigid said in unison as he retreated to his room, Charlie followed, close behind.

Linc pulled Brigid close. "I'm so glad I found you," he said as he wrapped his arm around her. He squeezed her tightly, as if John's story had touched him as much as it had Brigid.

Brigid was lost in thought, imagining such a beautiful love lost. Her heart broke for John and Francis, but she was happy that at least they'd been able to have each other for the time they did. Not everyone got to have a love like that.

Some people searched their whole lives and never had a chance to experience it. She felt that real and pure love like that was rare in this day and age. She wished she'd have been able to see John and Francis together.

"So am I," she said as she cuddled up under his arm. "I can't imagine my life without you in it."

"And I feel the same," Linc said as he kissed the top of her head.

*****

"How are things going in Cottonwood Spring, Fiona?" Brigid asked her sister after she'd answered Brigid's call. It was the following morning, and she'd felt the need to call her little sister to check in with her.

"Not too bad, although I have had the worst case of heartburn you could ever believe," Fiona grumbled.

Brigid was sitting on the edge of the bed, waiting for Linc to get out of the shower. She was rubbing aloe on her legs to help with all the sun she'd gotten at the beach the day before. She wasn't sunburned, but her skin had definitely gotten pink.

"I bet you're feeling miserable," Brigid commiserated. "How's the morning sickness?"

"Still with me," Fiona admitted. "About the only things I can eat are oatmeal and crackers, unless I want to spend the day hugging the toilet."

"Wow, that's terrible. So I probably shouldn't tell you how great of a time I'm having?" Brigid asked, wincing.

"No, please. Tell me. Maybe it will take my mind off my rebellious digestive system," Fiona groaned.

Brigid told Fiona all about the B & B where they were staying and how John and his dog, Charlie, had quickly become their friends. She went on to tell her all about their evening at the River Walk and then their day on Padre Island. She couldn't help but gush over each and every detail.

"Why didn't you try out surfing with Linc, you old fuddy-duddy?" Fiona asked. "I would love to see pictures of you on a surfboard."

"Ha-ha," Brigid said. "You know how uncoordinated I am. I wasn't about to spend money just to keep falling off of some stupid surfboard for a couple hours."

Fiona laughed. "True. Have you guys gone to see the Alamo yet? I know that's something you've always wanted to do," she said.

"Not yet, but it's on our list of things to do. I've been really surprised at how much there is to see here in San Antonio. I swear there isn't this much to see back home," Brigid said.

"That's because there isn't. Nobody comes to Cottonwood Springs for much besides skiing or snowboarding. People go to San Antonio because it's warm, beautiful, and historic," Fiona pointed out.

"I think it's beautiful in Cottonwood Springs," Brigid objected. "Although everything is just different here."

"What are your plans for today?" Fiona asked. "Horseback riding on a beach? A candlight dinner under the stars?" she teased.

"No, today we're going to this place called Natural Bridge Caverns," she said.

"A cave?" Fiona asked, shocked. "You're going underground? Why?"

"To see all the pretty rock formations, of course," Brigid said. "They also have more than just the caves, you know."

"Oh?" Fiona asked. "Like what?"

"They have one of those zipline canopy challenges, and a mining spot where you can search for gems and such. They even have a maze you can go through and a place to watch bats when they come out of the cave at sundown."

Brigid was pretty sure Fiona would be surprised at her willingness to visit something like a cave. She'd never really been interested in that sort of thing when they were growing up, but when Linc had found it online, it sounded like fun.

"You on a zipline?" Fiona scoffed. "I wish I was there to see that. Uh, who are you, and why do you sound like my sister?"

Brigid laughed. "Well, maybe I can get a picture for you. That is if I don't chicken out."

"Nah, you won't chicken out," Fiona encouraged. "I know you. Once you set your mind to something, you do it."

"Yeah, but those things usually don't include hanging by a thin wire and whizzing through the air. I'm not so sure I won't get up there and then have to climb back down," Brigid admitted.

"Well, even if you do, at least you tried," Fiona said. "That's all that matters."

The bathroom door opened and Linc walked out smelling fresh from his shower. He mouthed, "Who are you talking to?"

"Fiona," Brigid mouthed back.

"Hi, Fiona," Linc called out as he began to search for a pair of socks. He was wearing his favorite jeans and a casual grey t-shirt.

"Hi, Linc," Fiona called back. "Well, I better let you go so you can get back to your honeymoon. Make sure you bring me back something really cool and expensive," Fiona joked.

"Of course. Only the best for my sister," Brigid said with a laugh before she ended the call.

"How's she doing?" Linc asked as Brigid tossed her phone on the bed beside her.

"Still has morning sickness, but she seems to be in good spirits," she said. "I kind of feel bad that I'm not there to take her crackers or soup."

Linc moved around the bed and stood before her. Cupping her chin, he tilted her head upward. "She'll be fine. And you know she wouldn't want you fretting over her. There will be plenty of time for all of that when the baby comes. Then you can pamper her and the baby all at once." He smiled reassuringly at her.

"I have to admit I'm kind of looking forward to it," Brigid admitted. She stood up and gave Linc a hug. They stood together, their arms wrapped around each other for several long moments, simply enjoying being in each other's arms and feeling the warmth of the other.

"Are you about ready to go?" Linc asked.

"Almost," Brigid said. "I just need to finish putting on my makeup."

Not long after that they gave Charlie some ear scratches and waved goodbye to John who was tending to the flowers around the B & B. It felt a little strange to Brigid to be running around and doing so much, but it was a nice change of pace from sitting in a chair editing day after day. As they headed to their next adventure, Brigid clasped Linc's hand in hers and looked at him with a blissful, happy smile on her face.

CHAPTER TEN

Celine Aguirre had just about had enough of her husband. He was forever dismissing her job as a hobby and now that she thought about it, he'd never taken her seriously. Even when she'd gotten her degree in history, he'd asked her why she'd spent so much time on something completely worthless.

At the time, she thought that was his half-hearted way of trying to get her to strive for something higher. But the reality was, she didn't want anything else. She wanted a job bringing history to life. Was that really so terrible?

Over the seventeen years they'd been together, she'd slowly become someone she didn't recognize anymore. Celine visited a therapist on a regular basis and was on a few different medications, mostly to help improve her mood. She'd been depressed for so long she'd forgotten what it felt like to be happy.

Not that she'd realized it at first. It wasn't until she'd noticed that she didn't want to do anything she used to enjoy that she thought maybe she had a problem. After that, she'd secretly made an appointment with a therapist and started taking steps to change things. It had been a slow process, but that was all before Mark.

Celine stood up from her desk and walked out of her office with the intention of doing her normal rounds. She didn't like being one of those bosses who stays in their office and doesn't get involved with their staff. No, she preferred to be out there with them, making sure there weren't any issues that needed her attention, and that the Alamo was treated with the respect it deserved.

Her footsteps were quiet as she walked through the building and headed for the outer grounds. She didn't wear noisy high heels, just for the simple fact it helped keep the employees on their toes. There was a time when she hadn't been the boss, and she well remembered that loud shoes were a signal that someone was coming. Celine preferred to move quietly.

As she stepped out into the warm summer air, she thought about the first time she realized Mark was attracted to her. They'd been working together on a new idea for people who visited the Alamo for the haunted tours. She still remembered the way their hands had brushed against each other and the look in his eye when she gazed up at him. It had been so full of primal need it had taken her by surprise.

Nobody had ever looked at her that way before, and it had stirred something within her. It wasn't that she hadn't had lovers in her life, but none of them had been quite so passionate. She was the one who had always taken the initiative. She'd just thought she was one of those women who liked to take the lead.

Yet when Mark had initiated their relationship, it was the first time she'd actually felt like a woman. Someone who wanted to be taken care of rather than doing the taking. He'd kissed her, and there had been no holding back from then on. The sheer amount of desire she'd felt from a simple kiss had left her lightheaded and longing for more. And she knew he'd felt the same way.

Since then, they mainly rendezvoused at work, but once or twice they'd met for drinks after work. She'd end up driving them somewhere so they could be alone, and they'd make love in the back seat of her car. Occasionally, when she was feeling particularly down about herself, she'd call him to her office and they would lock the door. She knew it wasn't professional, and she never should have let it happen, but he made her feel young again. It was so wrong and yet it felt so right. It made her feel young, sexy, and still full of life.

She'd never taken risks like that before and the danger of getting caught just added to the excitement of it. After all, her husband barely looked at her anymore. The only times they were intimate, and those were few and far between, Celine felt as if it could be anyone lying with him. There was no more passion or lust. It was as if it was part of the job. Once they were finished, he'd roll over and pick up his phone, e-reader, or turn on the television. There was no cuddling or anything else to make her feel as though he still found her desirable.

Celine tried to maintain a purely professional air about her, but inside her heart had been shattered long ago. When Mark showed an interest in her, it was as if all the pieces had started to fit back together again. Before she knew it, she was smiling and singing in the car on the way to work. There were days when she wondered what Mark would do if she left her husband. She didn't want to scare him off, but her feelings for him were starting to grow.

What had started as a purely physical thing had quickly turned into something more for her. She was fairly confident that he felt the same way. Otherwise, why would he keep it going for this long? Surely, he had to have some sort of interest in her. If she left her husband, it wasn't like she expected Mark to marry her or anything, but she would like to explore what they had going on between them.

Of course, it would have to remain a secret. She knew she wouldn't be allowed to keep her job if it was revealed that she was having a romantic relationship with one of her employees. Maybe she could get a transfer or help Mark get a position somewhere else. There were always options if one knew where to look.

As soon as she walked outside, she began inspecting the courtyard. After all, it was the first thing every visitor to the Alamo saw, and she needed to make sure it was in top shape and would make a good impression on them. Looking around, Celine was satisfied it still looked presentable.

The grass could probably use a trim, but that was scheduled for later this week, which would be fine. Anyway, people weren't coming to the Alamo to see the grass, and it wasn't so shaggy that people would even notice it. She'd just learned a long time ago to spot issues before they became a problem. Staying ahead of things was a big part of her job.

As she rounded the corner of the building to check on the rest of the area, she heard people talking. The sounds were low and indistinct, but she could tell they were coming from one of the more secluded spots on the grounds.

She thought about leaving whoever it was to their conversation, but they'd had problems with teenagers recently wanting to hang out as if the Alamo was some kind of park. It was better to investigate now than have something trashed or vandalized. She slipped behind a line of trees and drew closer so she could see what was happening without bringing attention to herself.

The first thing she noticed was a gift shop employee's polo shirt. Whoever it was, the person worked at the Alamo. Since it wasn't normal for employees to hide out among the trees, she wanted to get a better look and see who it was. Depending on who it was, she might need to mention it to them later. When the person turned slightly, she recognized Zoey's profile.

So, she thinks she can slip away from her duties, hmm? Celine thought. *I wonder what she's doing? I better keep an eye on her and whoever else is out here with her to make sure this isn't something that needs to be addressed.*

Celine continued to watch, curious as to what was going on. It could be something entirely harmless or it could be something that needed her attention right then and there. After all, the Alamo wasn't your average historic monument. It must be treated with respect and some of the younger employees needed to be reminded of that.

She'd noticed a tour guide's polo shirt on the other person, but that person was still hidden by the thick cover of the trees and shrubs. The shrubs had been planted for privacy, but right now, she wished she could see the other person. As she watched, the person reached out and softly touched Zoey's cheek. It was the large hand of a man.

It appeared Zoey was having some sort of a tryst out here in the seclusion of the trees. Celine almost stepped out to confront the girl but thought it might be better to see who was with her before she confronted Zoey in case they managed to slip away.

"She means nothing to me," a familiar voice said. "I was just trying to get in her good graces and things went a little too far. I'm sorry." Celine knew the voice, but was trying to convince herself she was wrong until the man stepped closer to Zoey. There was no mistaking it was Mark. She felt her heart drop as his words sunk in. He was seeing Zoey? And who else?

"Then why were you making love to her?" Zoey asked as a tear slipped down her cheek. Celine felt sick to her stomach. Zoey had caught Mark having sex with someone else? How many women was he seeing besides her?

"Things were happening with her before you and I got together, babe. Like I said, I was just playing along so I could get the promotion. Then maybe you and I could get a place together? What do you think?" he asked as he leaned forward and began to kiss and fondle her. Rage boiled up in Celine as she realized they were talking about her. Zoey must have spied on their impromptu love-making in Celine's office. That was the only explanation. Well, at least Zoey hadn't reported it. Yet.

"Promise me you'll break it off with Celine," Zoey sniffled.

"I promise," he said as he wiped away another tear. "I told you, that old bag means nothing to me. You're the one I want."

Celine turned on her heel and slipped away. She felt the blood rushing to her face, pounding in her ears, and making it impossible to think rationally. Pure rage pumped through her veins. Mark had used her. He'd taken advantage of a lonely woman so he could get a promotion. She wanted to scream and cry. Actually, she wanted to beat him to a bloody pulp. But none of that would do her the least bit of good.

In the end, she knew there was no way she could let him get away with this. He'd used her, plain and simple. She'd put her heart on the line, and he'd ripped it from her chest and stomped on it. Well no more. She took a few deep breaths to calm herself before entering the office building. There was no way she'd let anyone see she was upset. She wouldn't give Mark that satisfaction.

She headed to her office, deciding she'd had enough of men and their games. Who was he to think he could play her emotions like that? He didn't know who he was messing with. The old, sad Celine was gone and in her place was a woman of substance. Like a phoenix rising from the ashes of her old self, something new had been born. He had no idea who he'd trifled with.

She'd make sure Mark knew how much he'd messed up. He'd find out he'd double-crossed the wrong woman.

CHAPTER ELEVEN

As Brigid and Linc approached the Alamo, Brigid was surprised by its beauty. Although it was over three hundred years old, the wooden doors and some of the more intricate details were amazing. It was almost as if they'd been carved yesterday, but she was sure some parts of the Alamo had been recreated. She knew nothing beyond the obvious about its history. She was hoping to learn more about it today.

"We need to hurry to meet up with our tour group. It's getting close to the time it said in the email," Linc said as he urged her forward. Linc had reserved their time with a tour group online the night before, which had made Brigid breathe a bit easier. She'd been worried about lines and having to wait for a long time in order to get in. This was far more efficient. They saw a tour guide waiting nearby and a group of people collecting around her.

"Good morning," the guide said. She was a gorgeous African American woman with high cheekbones and light brown eyes. Her smile was bright and infectious. Brigid couldn't help but like her immediately. "My name is Shavonne, and I'll be your guide this morning. If you've already purchased your tickets online, please have your proof of purchase ready. If you haven't, you can do so at the ticket office."

Linc pulled up the email on his phone and they waited for their turn. It all went fairly quickly and before long they were starting the tour.

As they walked through the Alamo, Brigid couldn't help but feel the history of it in the rough stone walls. She had a sense of all of the people who had lived and died here before the modern world built up around it.

There wasn't as much inside as she'd expected, a few display cases in some rooms and flags on display, yet it felt complete. It was almost magical. She and Linc didn't speak, remaining silent as they continued the tour. Brigid thought it was kind of like having a religious experience.

Eventually they made it back outside. The fresh air of the courtyard was welcome as they continued on the tour. Tall, lush trees shaded parts of the area from the intensity of the sun that was slowly rising in the sky. Brigid could feel sweat rolling down her lower back as she fanned herself with a brochure she'd picked up.

"This area is called the Arcade," the tour guide began. It was like a long outdoor hallway with no ceiling, only wooden beams crossing above it. There was a rock wall on one side with arches that had metal gates attached to them. In the early morning sun, it was beautiful. The greenery made the area look inviting, as if there should be a few tables and chairs set out for people to sit at and have a cup of coffee while they read their newspapers.

As the tour guide continued to point out different parts of the area she paused, "Excuse me one minute, folks," she said. Brigid had been busy looking around, but at the tour guide's words she craned her neck to see what had caused the guide to stop.

Someone was sitting in one of the archway areas, just off the path. It looked like it was someone who worked at the Alamo, since the person was wearing the same style of shirt as Shavonne, their tour guide. The person's back was to the group, so that only the person's shoulders were visible from where the group was standing. It was almost as if the person had chosen that particular spot to sit down and relax while they were on a break.

"Mark, what are you doing?" the tour guide asked as she drew closer to the person. "You know you can't hang out here," she began as she touched his shoulder. Brigid was watching the woman's face as she took in the man's appearance. Her eyes became wide before she let out a blood-curdling scream. She pulled her hand back quickly, not wanting to touch him. "Someone, call 911!" she yelled.

The members of the group began to look around at each other, clearly confused. Brigid pushed to the front with Linc close behind. She hurried to the guide's side to see if there was anything she could do. Shavonne was visibly trembling and was having trouble holding herself together.

"Oh my god," Brigid said when she saw the man's bloodied chest. She turned away quickly. She'd seen enough to know what had happened. The blood stain and his unnatural pallor indicated that the man was dead.

Three people came rushing over. One looked like he was a groundskeeper, and the other two appeared to be security. They said something to Shavonne while she was trying to collect herself.

"I'm sorry, but we're going to have to cut the tour short. Please follow me to the main hall. We'll give you all full refunds. Right this way," she said. Although her complexion was dark, her face had attained an unnatural pallor. Her eyes were watery and her lower lip trembled uncontrollably.

"Did you see that?" Brigid whispered to Linc.

"Yeah, that guy's been shot," Linc said, clearly in shock. His eyes were wide with surprise. Brigid had almost gotten used to seeing lifeless bodies. Not that she was proud of the fact, but she'd forgotten that Linc hadn't been with her the other times when she'd discovered a murder victim. Still, the eerie stillness of the man's lifeless body was unsettling.

Brigid nodded. "I wonder what happened to him," she began. She ran her hand along Linc's arm, trying to help him focus on something else.

"Oh, no. I know that look. Don't even think about it. Let the police do their job. You're here on our honeymoon, remember?" Linc said warily. His color was starting to come back, which was good. She was worried Linc was going to pass out or get sick.

"Yeah, I know," Brigid sighed, but she couldn't get the image of the man out of her mind. What had Shavonne said his name was? Mark? Their group was directed away from the scene and led to where they were issued refunds and given vouchers to the gift shop.

Many in their tour group wasted no time leaving the Alamo. They'd seen more than enough and were afraid they might get caught up in the investigation. As the room began to empty, a police officer took Shavonne to the side and asked her a few questions before walking away. Brigid watched the interaction and waited until they had finished.

"I think we should go," Linc began. "Maybe we can see what else is around here. I think I saw a wax museum nearby."

"Wait a minute. I want to make sure our tour guide's okay," Brigid said, nodding in her direction. "And I'd like to visit the gift shop. Maybe I can use the voucher they gave us for some souvenirs or something. Might as well put it to good use."

Linc gave her a look that said he wasn't buying it, but he nodded anyway.

Brigid approached Shavonne, "Excuse me. I'm sorry to bother you, are you alright?" she asked gently.

The woman nodded. "Yeah, I think so. I just can't believe anyone would do something like this," she said sniffling. She brushed a few tears off her cheeks.

"Do the police suspect foul play?" Brigid asked carefully.

Shavonne nodded. "I think so. I mean, I'm sure they're going to explore all the possibilities. It's not like Mark would have a reason to do this to himself." She shivered, running her hands over her arms. "I used to think this place was safe."

"I'm sure it is," Brigid reassured. "Were you two friends?"

The woman shrugged. "As friendly as co-workers are, you know? I didn't hate the guy. Oh, I just remembered something. I think he was seeing a girl from the gift shop. She must be a wreck. Poor Zoey," she said shaking her head.

"Take care of yourself," Brigid said as she walked away. She looked over at Linc who was busy examining something in a display case, so she hurried over to the nearest officer. "Excuse me, do you think the young man was murdered?"

"I'm sorry, but I'm not at liberty to discuss it," he said apologetically.

"Have you spoken to his girlfriend in the gift shop?" she asked. That seemed to get the officer's attention.

"He has a girlfriend that works here?" he asked, then he said, "Come with me." He began to speak into his radio calling someone named Detective Brewer to meet him outside. Brigid looked over at Linc who was watching her leave with the officer.

"What did you do?" Linc mouthed. Brigid just shrugged, and he followed them at a distance.

A man who looked to be somewhere in his late forties or early fifties met them outside the wooden doors. He wasn't in uniform. Instead, he wore a blue and white plaid shirt and a pair of slacks. He extended his hand to Brigid.

"My name is Detective Brewer. My officer tells me you have

information about the deceased."

Brigid shook his hand and then cleared her throat. "My name's Brigid Olson. I found out the man has a girlfriend who works in the gift shop. Her name is Zoey," she offered.

"And you know this how?" he asked as he began writing in his notebook.

"I spoke to the tour guide," she said simply. Detective Brewer gave the officer a long disapproving look before turning back to Brigid.

"You spoke to the tour guide?" he repeated.

Brigid shrugged. "People just tell me things. That's why I help out on criminal cases where I'm from."

"Do you now?" the detective said as he tapped his pen on his teeth. "And where are you from?" he asked, his pen hovering over the notebook.

"Cottonwood Springs, Colorado," Brigid said. "I assist the sheriff, his name is Corey Davis, with verifying alibis and things of that nature. I'd be more than happy to offer my assistance," she said easily.

Detective Brewer seemed to really look at Brigid then. "I appreciate that Ms…"

"Mrs. Brigid Olson," she offered.

"Mrs. Olson, I hope you understand, but I can't just take your word for it. I'd need to speak with this Sheriff Davis first, and it would help if you knew someone locally who worked with the police department to vouch for you as well," he said eyeing her.

"Of course," she said as she pulled out her cell phone. She quickly found Corey Davis' number and hit send.

"Hey Brigid," he said after a few rings. "I thought ya' was on yer' honeymoon."

"I am. Long story short, there's been a murder, and I need you to speak to this detective. Let him know I can help, would you?" she asked.

"Sheesh, Brigid, only you can go on yer' honeymoon and end up helpin' with a murder investigation," he sighed. "I'm sure Linc ain't too happy about this, but put the detective on the phone."

Brigid handed the phone over to the detective who took it, looking surprised. He walked a few steps away, and spoke with Sheriff Davis for a few moments before turning back and handing her the phone.

"Sheriff Davis spoke highly of you," he said simply. "You wouldn't happen to have anyone on your phone that's a local cop, would you?"

"Actually, I do have someone," she said touching her finger to her chin.

"The B & B we're staying at is run by one of your own who's retired. His name is John," Linc offered as he stepped forward. Brigid smiled up at him.

"I know John," the detective said. "So you think he'll speak highly of you if I call him?" Detective Brewer asked. Brigid nodded. "I believe so," she said.

Detective Brewer sighed. "Well, you got more information than my guys did in half the time. With a murder taking place at a high-profile location like this, I'm going to need all the help I can get to wrap it up quickly. Don't go bragging to the press, though," he said finally. He seemed reluctant, but grateful, for whatever help she might be able to provide.

"No problem," Brigid said nodding. "My lips are sealed." She understood. The police never wanted details leaked to the press before they were able to find the murderer. Otherwise, it made their job just that much harder.

"Great. Sheriff Davis said you're good at finding suspects. If you can ask around and get me a list, I'd be grateful. Here's my card," he said as he pulled one from his wallet. Give me a call when you have something."

Brigid nodded as she took it. "Not a problem. I promise you won't regret this," she said.

"I hope not," Detective Brewer said as he walked towards the crime scene.

Brigid sighed. Somehow, she'd once again found herself in the middle of a murder investigation. At least this time, the victim wasn't someone she knew.

CHAPTER TWELVE

"Brigid, I really don't think you should get involved in this," Linc said apprehensively. They were standing in the courtyard of the Alamo, the sun getting higher in the sky. His face was filled with concern. "Let's go get some lunch or something. Let these guys do their job, and we'll stay out of their way."

"Linc, you know I can't leave this alone. Think about this poor man's family and friends. There have to be people who care about him. You know how hard the sheriff's department back home works, and Cottonwood Springs is just a small little town. Can you imagine how overworked these guys are? Not to mention all the other stuff they're dealing with. The police are human, too.

"If I can help in any way...," she let her sentence trail off, her face bunched in worry. She had so much sympathy for law enforcement. It was a hard job that often didn't get much praise. If she could help, even in the slightest way, she felt it was her way to give back to the community.

"I know. You feel that you need to help," he sighed. He ran his hand down his face and turned away, pacing slightly. Brigid could see he was deep in thought. He always did that when he was carefully weighing his options about something. Linc may have been a thrill seeker but he wasn't reckless. There was nothing he disliked more than being uncertain.

As he paced back and forth across the pavement, Brigid wondered if she'd be able to just drop the investigation if he insisted. She loved him more than anything, but doing these sorts of investigations had gotten into her blood. It wouldn't be easy to walk away from it if he refused to support her. But she also knew there was no way she could go against him. If he truly wanted her to stay out of it, she'd have to find a way to be okay with it.

Relationships were all about give and take. There was no way she wanted to start their marriage with a fight just because she wanted to get involved in something that had nothing to do with her besides being in the right place at the wrong time. When he turned back to her, she held her breath in anticipation

"When we finish this, can we get back to our honeymoon?"

Brigid could see the worry on his face and felt terrible for putting him in this position. It wasn't as if she went around looking for people who'd been murdered, but once she discovered a murder, she felt she had to do something to help solve the crime. It felt like it was her duty.

"Yes, absolutely," she nodded. "We find the suspects, get their alibis, and see what shakes loose. After that, we focus totally on you and me." She stepped forward and put her hand on his chest before giving him a kiss. "I promise."

"Okay, then," he agreed with a sigh. "I don't want to try to change you, and this is a part of who you are. I knew it when I married you, and so I have to stay true to my word as well as to you. Let's do this investigation."

"You mean, you're going to help?" Brigid asked surprised. Linc had helped out the first time she'd been involved in a murder, but since that one he'd mostly been a cheerleader. To have him by her side was really something.

"Of course. Although we probably should have put this sort of thing in our vows. In sickness and in health, through murder investigations and kidnapping cases, till death do us part," he said with a laugh.

"Thank you, Linc," Brigid said, relieved. She felt the tension in her shoulders melt away. "I don't know if I could have relaxed if I didn't try to help even a little. It's almost like it was a sign. What are the odds that we show up here and are on the tour when a murder victim is found?"

"I know, which is one of the things I love about you," he said with a smile. "You're so selfless and brave, although sometimes a little too brave," he said, raising an eyebrow. "But you have a heart of gold, and I know you only want to help."

"I have no idea what you're talking about," Brigid said easily, even though she knew exactly what he was referring to. "I don't do brave stuff," she scoffed. There had been a couple of times when she'd simply reacted without any thought for her own safety. It was a bad habit, but it had also helped her catch the bad guy more than once. Who knows how many times sheer luck had kept her out of harm's way?

"I think we should give the police officials a little bit of space, though. You don't want to step on anyone's toes or get in the way," Linc suggested. "Looks like they have quite a bit going on right now. We wouldn't want to accidentally mess up the murder scene while they're looking for clues."

"You're right," Brigid said as she looked at all of the people in uniform who were milling around. "Let's go back to the B & B and get something to eat. I want to grab my notebook, so I can keep everything straight. These aren't people I know, so there will be a lot of names I'll have to remember." She wrapped her hand around Linc's arm, and they started to walk out to the parking lot.

"I'm starting to think you like this sort of thing," Linc said as they walked together. "I've always wondered why you take a notebook with you wherever you go. Now I know. It's in case you happen to find someone murdered."

"I don't like it that someone was murdered, Linc," she chastised. "And I always carry a notebook. You never know when you may want to write something down."

"I'm not saying you like it when people are murdered, but I think you do like doing this private eye stuff. And honestly? You're pretty good at it," he said, almost proudly.

"Why thank you," Brigid said with a grin. "Maybe I just have one of those faces people like to tell stuff to. But I still really love being an editor, you know that."

"Maybe," Linc said. "But you're a natural at this investigation stuff. Maybe you missed your true calling."

Brigid opened her mouth to answer him, but she was cut short by the sound of someone crying out. They both turned to see what the commotion was. A young woman was being supported by an officer. Her grief was so overwhelming, she was having trouble standing up. Brigid's heart melted for the woman who must have been close to the victim. Her hair was hanging down in her face as her body tried to collapse. She shook with emotion.

"That poor girl," Brigid said. She wondered what the relationship was between the girl and the victim. Her mind wanted to find out, so she could put the pieces together. She wanted to ask the young woman questions and see if she could help find justice for her friend.

An older woman in a pantsuit moved toward the young woman and placed her hand on her shoulder.

"Don't you dare touch me!" she screamed. The older woman raised her hands as if to show she meant no harm and backed away. "You did this, didn't you?" the girl screamed. "You knew he couldn't ever love a shriveled-up old woman when he had me, so you killed him. You killed him! How could you?" she cried out as she began to collapse again.

It was as if it had taken all her strength to lash out at the woman and then she was spent. The officer who was holding her walked her to a nearby bench in the shade where she could sit down, probably so he wouldn't have to continue holding her up. The girl continued sobbing which could be heard across the courtyard.

"I just want to..." Brigid began as she turned to Linc, and he shook his head. He didn't need her to finish her sentence. Her intentions were as plain on her face as if they were written there.

"Go ahead. I'll be in the car cooling it down. Try not to take too long. We want to head to the B & B and get back here before everyone leaves," he said.

"I won't. I just want to talk to her and find out who she is. Maybe I can help her calm down a little and let her know I'll be doing what I can to find out who did this. She's obviously close to the victim. I'd like to see if I can give her a little peace of mind," she said carefully. "How can I walk away when the girl's so distraught?" He nodded as she started to walk towards the bench where the young girl was sitting.

Brigid watched as the detective signaled for the older woman to join him. He obviously wanted to know what that entire scene was about and intended to question her first. The older woman looked conflicted about staying with the girl or doing what the detective had asked her to do.

She finally turned and walked slowly towards the detective, as if she wasn't looking forward to the conversation that was about to take place. The officer who had helped the young girl walked away, leaving her sniffling by herself, and sitting on the bench.

"Excuse me," Brigid said as she approached the girl. "Are you okay?"

The young woman looked up with big, red-rimmed eyes. Tears were still streaming down her flushed cheeks, even though she'd managed to collect herself slightly. She'd started hiccupping from her crying, reminding Brigid of a small child.

"No," the young woman said. "Someone murdered my boyfriend." Her voice was weak and wobbly.

"I heard you yelling at that woman," Brigid began. "Do you think she was the one who did it?"

The girl looked Brigid up and down warily. "You don't look like a cop, so why do you care?"

"Actually, I'm helping with the case. Kind of like a private investigator," she said, thinking about what Linc had said. "I do a separate investigation from the police, and then we come together and see what we have." She stuck out her hand. "My name's Brigid."

That seemed to satisfy the girl. "Zoey," she said as she shook her hand. "Yeah, I do think it was her."

Brigid wanted to ask her a few questions, but she knew Linc would be waiting for her. "Are you going to be here for a while? I need to get a few things, but I'll be back in a little while," she said.

The girl nodded. "Yeah, I'll be here. I work in the gift shop, but I don't think any of us will be going anywhere for a while."

"Good. Please don't leave until I get back. I want to help find whoever did this and make sure they pay for it," Brigid said.

The girl looked slightly taken aback but nodded. "Okay, I'll be here. Just don't take all day. As soon as they say I can leave, I will. Right now, I don't know if I can ever come back to this place again."

"I won't," Brigid promised as she stood up. Looking around, she noticed more tour guides and what she assumed were gift shop workers collecting in the courtyard.

Any one of them could have done it, Brigid thought. *It could be any one of them, or none of them at all. It could have been a crime of passion or just a random attack.*

She looked down at Zoey's stony expression. She knew that even though the girl looked very upset, it could all be an act. She didn't know these people like she'd known the people back home. Any one of them could be capable of murder. She'd learned the hard way that people were capable of just about anything. Brigid only hoped she wasn't in over her head as she headed for the parking lot.

CHAPTER THIRTEEN

Brigid and Linc arrived at the Silver Star B & B just as John was finishing up with the lawnmower. Charlie was looking rather bored while lying on the porch, but he perked up when he saw Brigid and Linc walk up to the house.

"What have you two been up to this morning?" John asked merrily as he climbed off the riding mower. His shirt had a ring of sweat, and he looked a little flushed.

"We found ourselves in a bit of a situation, I'm afraid," Brigid admitted. "We were on our tour of the Alamo, and someone was found murdered."

"Are you serious?" he asked as he brushed beads of sweat from his forehead with his sleeve. "That's a new one. Who's investigating?"

"Detective Brewer," Brigid said. "I managed to convince him to let me help. I just couldn't stay out of it. I've done so much of this type of thing back home I couldn't let it go."

"I understand. Once you get bitten by the bug, there's no going back," he said with a sly smile. "What are you going to do to help?"

"I'll go get your notebook," Linc interjected before kissing the side of her head and slipping inside.

"I'm going to gather a list of suspects and question them. Usually something shakes loose with that," she explained. She'd begun wondering on the drive to the B & B if she'd bitten off more than she could chew. After all, she was used to investigating a crime when there were people she knew. Here everyone was a stranger. She wasn't sure if that would be a help or a hindrance.

Granted, she knew nothing about these people, so she could be completely objective about people's involvement. But at the same time, she was afraid she might miss something for the same reason.

"Sounds like you could use Charlie here," John began. "That's his field of expertise."

"Oh?" Brigid asked as the dog trotted over, having heard his name. He looked more than happy to be included in the conversation.

"Yes, ma'am. He had the regular training police dogs get for sniffing out things, but he always had this uncanny ability to know when someone was lying. He'd whine a little and lick my hand if he knew the person in question was telling a fib." He looked down at the dog and gave him a scratch.

"He's actually still able to do police work. They know him down at the station, and they trust him. Why don't you take him with you when you question your suspects? Not only can he help you tell if a person is lying to you, but it would be much safer. You never know what a person is capable of, especially in this day and age. If someone kills once, they may be willing to do it again. He'll protect you with his life." John looked down fondly at the dog with a wistful smile. "I trust him completely."

"Are you sure?" Brigid asked just as Linc returned with her notebook. "You don't need him around here?"

"Nah," John said. "He could use a day out anyway. Please, I insist.

Anyway, I suspect he gets a little bored sitting around here with me all the time. Let me go get his official leash. He always knew he was on duty when he wore it." The older man walked into the B & B while Brigid waited. She gave Linc a quick rundown of what John had just told her about Charlie.

"It'll almost be like having Jett with us," Linc said with a grin. "Only in a lie detector version."

"Kind of," Brigid chuckled. "But in a smaller version. Hopefully this guy won't drool nearly as much. I swear, Jett drools more than I ever thought possible."

John returned with a leash that had "S.A.P.D." written across it in bright white lettering. As soon as Charlie saw it, he began to yip.

"I told you he loved it," John chuckled as he clipped the leash onto the dog's collar. "Now you help Brigid here find the bad guy. Okay, Charlie?" He handed the leash over to Brigid. "Go with her and help her sniff out the suspects."

Charlie moved over by Brigid and sat down beside her. He looked up at John attentively and then at Brigid as if he were saying, "I understand."

"You want to help me figure out who the bad guy is, Charlie?" Brigid asked him. He looked up at her and licked his lips. He wiggled a bit in place, as if he was too antsy to sit still.

John laughed. "I think that's a yes," he said. "Now like I said, he's been trained in the usual fashion. He will attack if instructed, and he can find scents if you give him a sample. But when you're questioning suspects, you make sure he's right beside you. He listens. If he just sits there like he is now, the person is telling the truth. If he starts bumping your hand with his nose, whining or trying to get your attention, they're lying.

"I don't know how he does it, and he wasn't trained that way. It's just something I figured out he could do. It sure helped on more than one case, which is why he's known to the older guys at the station. Brewer will recognize him, I'm sure. If anyone needs someone to vouch for you, send them my way. I'll set them straight. I still have a little pull down at the station."

"Thank you," Brigid said. "Truly. I really appreciate this. I feel a bit better knowing I have Charlie here. My dog at home is well trained, too. He's helped me out more times than I can count, so I know I can put my faith in Charlie here."

She reached down and gave the dog a gentle pat. It was reassuring to have a loyal dog at her feet once more. He may not be as big as her Newfoundland back home, but that didn't mean he didn't have a heart just as large. She'd seen that much in the short time she'd been at the B & B.

"Take care of him, and if he does a good job and helps you find the killer, you owe him a vanilla shake." John looked a little sheepish. "It's kind of a tradition. I always rewarded him for a job well done."

"That's not a problem," Linc said. "Sounds like a good idea, anyway. Ice cream after a long day is a reward I could get behind, too."

They waved to John and thanked him again before loading Charlie up in the car and heading back toward the Alamo.

"Do you think they'll give you a hard time since we're bringing him?" Linc asked as they drew closer.

"I don't think so," Brigid said after a moment. "After all, he is a police dog. John said Detective Brewer would know him when he saw him. I'm sure it'll be alright. Besides, he probably won't be the only police dog that will be called in."

"I hope so," Linc said. "I feel much better about this whole thing with our furry friend here tagging along. Whoever did this has a gun, Brigid. They killed a man with it, and we don't even know why. Maybe it was just a random incident."

Brigid gave Linc a pointed look. "Do you really think that after seeing that young woman this morning? She seemed convinced that other woman had done it."

"That could also just have been grief talking," he said. "As soon as something terrible happens people are always looking somewhere to place the blame. Sometimes humans can be senselessly violent for no real reason. Just because someone is murdered doesn't mean there has to be any real motive. The guy could have been in the wrong place at the wrong time or saw something he shouldn't have."

Brigid nodded. "That's true, but I don't think that's the case here. I bet we'll stir up all sorts of interesting information once we start asking a few questions. You know how it works. Besides, when people work together, they tend to get to know more about each other than they realize."

Linc sighed. "You're right. I hope for our sake and the sake of our honeymoon this ends up being an open and shut case. I'd like to have your focus be on you and me and not on this murder."

"I bet Charlie here will be a huge help," she said. "We'll find the murderer, won't we boy?"

Charlie gave a small yip and both Brigid and Linc laughed.

"I guess that's a yes from him, too," Linc said. "Honestly, he looks as if he's enjoying himself."

"Maybe he is. John said he knew what the leash meant. Maybe he misses doing doggie detective work. It's not like police dogs get to choose when they retire," Brigid pointed out.

"You've got a point there. Maybe he feels like he's still in his prime and he's ready to go?" Linc suggested. "I mean, who knows how old he is. Some people aren't made for retirement, maybe dogs are the same way."

"I guess we'll find out," Brigid sighed. "I just hope he still knows his old tricks."

CHAPTER FOURTEEN

As Brigid walked up the sidewalk to the Alamo with Linc on one side and Charlie on the other, she felt as if everyone was staring at them. Was it the fact they had Charlie with them or was it something else? Most of the people gave them a cursory glance before turning away, but Brigid could feel the weight of their gazes as they approached the entrance.

Perhaps it was the fact they were heading towards a murder scene, rather than trying to get away from it, like most people would want to do. Brigid tried not to let it rattle her as they drew closer. It didn't take long before Detective Brewer emerged from the crowd.

"Can I assume this is Charlie?" he asked as he joined them. He offered his hand to the dog who eagerly licked it.

"The one and only. John offered him to me. He thought he could help with the case," Brigid explained.

"Then you definitely have my blessing," he said sounding impressed. "We've kept all the workers here on site for now. It's my understanding that our team hasn't done much in the way of questioning yet, so please keep me informed on what you get. Send me a text or call as often as you need to. Everyone is supposed to be in their typical work location, but we've tried to keep them somewhat separated.

"We're still searching the grounds for a murder weapon. It appears he was shot sometime early this morning, around 6:30 or 7:00. We need to know where everyone was at that time, and if they have someone who can corroborate their story. We're almost finished in the main area, and then we're going to be moving to the parking lot to check their vehicles." He turned and looked around the area. "Did John tell you about Charlie's special skill?" he asked.

"Yes, he did," Brigid said nodding. "I'll let you know if he comes up with anything."

"Good. He's a great asset. I'm glad to have him on the case. Let me know if you need anything or something shakes loose." Detective Brewer turned on his heel and then disappeared back into the sea of uniforms.

"That guy's not the warmest human being I've ever met," Linc muttered.

"I'm sure he's just focused on his job. Come on, let's go meet Zoey first. She was the one I spoke to before we left. I want to see what she has to say." They turned and headed for the gift shop where an officer pushed the door open for them as they entered. Inside, behind the cash register, were Zoey and another young girl.

"Brigid, right?" Zoey said as she stood up. "You can't have dogs in here. Unless he's a service animal or whatever. Then he's fine."

Brigid shook her head. "He's a police dog. He's going to help me out today." She looked around the small room filled with shirts, coffee mugs, keychains, and magnets. "Is there anywhere we can talk privately?"

"I'll step outside," the other girl said quickly. She squeezed Zoey's shoulder as she walked by and stepped out the door.

"Let me get some chairs," Zoey offered as she disappeared into the back. Soon she reappeared with three folding chairs. They set them up in an open space near the register.

"My husband, Linc, and I are assisting the police department with investigating the murder that happened here," Brigid began. "How did you know the victim?"

"Mark and I had been dating for a little while now," Zoey said. "We met here at work."

Brigid began to take notes. It was a little different dealing with people she didn't know. "We saw you accuse a woman of murdering him. Can you explain why you think she did it?"

"Well, I mean, it's like this. I found out recently that Mark and Celine had been having an affair at the same time he was seeing me," Zoey began. "Isn't it usually the jealous lover who murders the guy? I figured she found out about us and was driven crazy with the thought of him being with another woman."

"By that description you're setting yourself up as a suspect, as well," Linc pointed out.

Brigid watched Charlie out of the corner of her eye. He was sitting up and attentive, apparently listening to every word Zoey said. So far, not even a flinch had come from him.

"Well, I guess that's true," she admitted. "But I didn't do it." She said it so simply it was as if she was stating the obvious. "I was mad when I first found out Mark was seeing that old bag, but I got to thinking about it, and we'd never really made it official. You know, like we were exclusive to each other. I planned on talking to him about it when I saw him today." Her lip began to tremble. "I couldn't ever hurt him."

"I understand, but we need proof of that. Can you tell me where you were between 6:30 and 7:00 this morning?" Brigid asked.

"Sure, that's easy. I was still at home. My roommate can vouch for me. We were cooking breakfast around that time," she shrugged.

"Okay, great. I'll pass that information on. Do you know of

anyone else besides Celine who might have a motive for killing Mark?" Brigid asked. Charlie had remained motionless the entire time she'd been talking to Zoey. She silently hoped he was still as good at this as he used to be.

Zoey shook her head. "Not that I can think of, right off. I mean, he and I had only gone out a couple of times, so I don't know his friends or anything. Nobody around here ever said anything bad about him that I can remember."

"That's okay. One last thing. Do you happen to own a gun?" she asked.

"No!" Zoey said quickly. "I hate the things. Never could stand them."

"I'm going to give you my cell phone number in case you remember something else. We're going to be around here for a while so give me a call if you think of anything else that might be helpful," Brigid said. "In the meantime, try to relax."

Zoey nodded and sniffled as a tear ran down her cheek. "I just can't believe he's gone, you know? Like, I keep expecting him to walk in at any moment and tell me it was all some kind of a twisted joke."

"I wish it was," Linc offered. "But I'm afraid it's not. Try to take care of yourself. Grieving is a rough process to go through. Take your time with it."

Brigid and Linc stood up. "Do you have any idea where Celine may be?" Brigid asked.

"Well, they told all of us to go to our regular work areas, so she's probably in her office," Zoey said. She began to gather up their chairs as Brigid and Linc stepped back outside. They told the other girl she could go back in, and she quietly slipped through the door.

"It looked like Charlie thought she was telling the truth," Linc said as they followed the sidewalk over to the building where the offices were located.

"It would appear so," Brigid agreed. "Hopefully he hasn't lost his touch, but he seemed to be listening."

Linc nodded. "I thought so, too. Let's go talk to this Celine woman and see what she has to say. Maybe Charlie will pick something up with her." He looked toward the officers who were all huddled together. "Looks like they must be done with the grounds. I bet they're moving to the parking lot now. My bet is they don't find anything there, either. After all, who'd keep a murder weapon in their car?"

Brigid shrugged. "I have no clue, but it's probably better to be safe than sorry. In my opinion, if someone did, they aren't a very good criminal, not that there's ever a good criminal."

CHAPTER FIFTEEN

Brigid raised her hand and knocked on the office door with the name "Celine Aguirre" on the nameplate. She looked over at Linc who gave her a reassuring smile. She felt odd about walking around behind the scenes at an historic monument like the Alamo. It was almost as if they were trespassing, even if they were on official business.

"Come in," a woman's voice called out. Turning the doorknob, Brigid stepped inside with Charlie in tow. Linc followed behind them and closed the door.

The older woman sitting behind a desk in the room looked tired and her eyes were red, as if she'd been crying. Brigid's heart went out to her. She obviously cared about the man who had been murdered. Of course, how could she not?

She seemed to be one of the higher-ups at the Alamo, and more than likely she had some familiarity with the victim, even if they weren't having an illicit affair. Brigid could remember the times she'd lost people she knew. It seemed like it was even more of a shock to the system when it had been sudden, like this one had.

"We've come to ask you a few questions, if you're up to it," Brigid said.

The woman nodded. "Sure, that's fine. Are you with the police?"

"Something like that," Brigid said. "I'm like a private investigator and help the police department with some of the leg work to free up their time. Identifying possible suspects, asking basic questions, things like that."

That seemed to be enough for Celine, who sat back in her chair. She looked as though she was already exhausted and the day had only just started. "I hope they find what they're looking for and let us go soon. This whole thing is like a nightmare. I'm ready to go home and curl up with a carton of ice cream."

She ran her fingers under her eyes, fixing her smudged makeup slightly. "I feel as if I've run a marathon, and yet all I've been doing is sitting here in my office."

"I can't say that I blame you," Brigid responded. "My name's Brigid and this is Linc," she said gesturing to her husband. "And this guy is Charlie," she said as she gave him a pet. "He's a K-9 officer with the San Antonio Police Department." Brigid didn't feel the need to let her know he was retired. That piece of information didn't seem all that relevant.

"Nice to meet you," Celine said. "I'm Celine Aguirre, Director here at the Alamo. How can I help you? I'm afraid I don't know much about what happened. They asked me to look around the crime scene to make sure nothing was out of place, but I couldn't do it."

"I can't say that I blame you. It must be tough knowing one of your employees was murdered right here on the grounds," Brigid said.

"It is. I keep wondering if there is something I could have done differently. Maybe I should have had more security or had them come in earlier. Something," she said wistfully.

"Hindsight is always 20/20," Linc offered. "I'm sure you did the best you could with the knowledge you had at the time. Don't beat yourself up over it."

"I suppose you're right," she said. "It still feels as though somehow I'm indirectly responsible." She sighed and then cleared her throat. "Anyway, you said you had questions?"

"Yes, I do. First of all, I'd like to ask you about your relationship with the victim, Mark," Brigid began. "I overheard what that young woman, Zoey, said about you a little while ago. That's a pretty hefty accusation." She leaned towards Celine, watching Charlie out of the corner of her eye for any changes.

Celine seemed as though she was pretty torn up about the murder, but that didn't mean it wasn't all an act. Brigid didn't know this woman or what she was capable of.

"Well I guess it won't do any good to try to hide it now," she sighed. "Yes, Mark and I were having an affair. It hadn't been going on very long. Maybe a few months, if that."

Brigid nodded. "Did you know he was also in a relationship with Zoey?"

"I had recently become aware of it, yes," Celine admitted. Her words were clipped, as if she were trying to bite back her anger.

"Had you said anything about it to Mark?" Brigid asked as she took a few notes. Finding out your lover was seeing someone else was more than enough motive for some people to commit murder.

"I left a note in his locker last night. I'd been trying to decide what I was going to say and do. I hadn't realized that he and I weren't exclusive. I guess I just assumed that since we were having an affair," she sighed and a single tear began to slip down her cheek before she brushed it away. "I guess these days that doesn't matter. Times have definitely changed, haven't they?"

"So you were mad at him," Brigid said. "Is that what you're saying?"

Celine looked thoughtful for a moment. "At first I was, yes. But I didn't kill him if that's what you're implying."

"That's not what I'm trying to get at," Brigid said gently, noting how still Charlie was sitting. Celine had just said she didn't kill Mark and Charlie hadn't even moved. Obviously, he didn't think she was being untruthful.

"I'm trying to wrap my head around who he was and who may have been in a position to want harm to come to him," Brigid said. "I need to understand the type of person he was in order for me to identify anyone who may have had a motive to want to see him come to some sort of harm." She crossed her legs. "Can you think of anyone who would have had a desire to hurt him?"

"One of our other tour guides wasn't happy I was appointing Mark to a new position. An older gentleman by the name of Jerry Martinez seemed to think he should have gotten it instead," she sniffed.

"Is he here today?" Brigid asked, jotting down the name.

"Yes, I believe he is," Celine nodded. "Although I highly doubt Jerry would do something like that, but still. You just never know with people sometimes."

"Anyone else?" Linc asked as Brigid was writing.

"Well, maybe," Celine said as she thought. "Last week there was this big guy who stopped Mark one evening while we were leaving the building. Mark seemed to know who the guy was because he told me to go on ahead so he could talk to him. But I didn't like the looks of the guy."

"Why's that?" Brigid asked. "Could you describe him?"

"I can do better than that," Celine said as she pulled out her cell phone. "I took a picture of Mark and him while they were talking. Like I said, I had a feeling there was something up with him." She swiped on her phone for a while before turning it to show Brigid.

The photo was slightly grainy, but it was still good enough that Brigid could see him. The guy was fairly big and looked tough. Not exactly the kind of guy you wanted to mess with.

"Would you send me that picture?" Brigid asked. She gave Celine her cell number and the woman pressed send. "Thank you, that's extremely helpful. I can pass this along to the detective handling this case. I'm sure he'll be able to figure out who the man in the photo is."

"Do you think he did this?" Celine asked. "Do you think he murdered Mark?"

"I have no idea. That's what we're trying to find out," Brigid said. "Would you mind telling me where you were between 6:30 and 7:00 this morning?"

Celine steepled her fingers as she sat back in her chair. "I believe I was at home getting ready for work. I leave the house around 6:45 on average. Sometimes a little sooner, sometimes a little later."

"Is there anyone who can verify that?" Brigid asked as she took note of what Celine said.

"I don't think so," Celine said nervously. "Oh, wait. I'm sure there are security cameras outside of our apartment building. They probably caught me going to my car." She seemed relieved to have proof. Meanwhile Charlie was simply listening with mild interest.

"I'm sure you understand that I have to ask everyone that question. The police department will follow up and verify it," Brigid said as the office door opened and Detective Brewer stepped inside.

"Celine Aguirre?" he asked. When she nodded, he continued, "You're under arrest for the murder of Mark Muller."

"What? But I didn't...," she sputtered as he began to read Celine

106

her rights. She turned to Brigid with wide eyes. "I didn't do it."

"We found what we believe to be the murder weapon in your car. Forensics will test it to be certain, but it appears to be the same kind of gun the coroner thinks was used to murder the victim. Do you admit to owning a handgun?" he asked.

"My husband and I have one at home in our safe, but I can't even remember the combination for it," she said, tears streaming down her face. She turned and looked at Brigid with a look of horror. "I'm not the one who murdered Mark!"

Another officer came into the room and led Celine away in handcuffs. Brigid stood and placed her hand on the retreating detective's arm. "Detective, I really don't think she did it."

"Why's that?" he asked with a tone in his voice that sounded as if he was humoring her. Brigid could tell from his slight smirk he didn't believe her. She refused to let his attitude phase her.

"Well for one thing, Charlie didn't even flinch the whole time we were talking to her. Even when she plainly said she didn't kill him," she pointed out.

"Brigid's right," Linc offered. "She sounded pretty convincing, too. She also gave us two more suspects. One was an unknown guy who stopped Mark just outside the Alamo when he was leaving after work, not too long ago."

Brigid held up her phone and showed the detective the photograph of the man. A look of recognition slid over his face. "That's the bartender over at El Lobo," he said meeting Brigid's eyes. "I've suspected him of being the new muscle for an illegal gambling ring that operates in this area."

He paused as if he were considering that Celine may not have done it. "It's not looking good for her. If forensics comes back and says that it was the weapon used in the murder, and since we found it in her car, that's almost like a signed confession."

"But why would a guilty woman allow you to search her car, knowing that the murder weapon was in there?" Linc asked.

Brigid nodded in agreement. "That doesn't sound like something a person would do if they'd committed murder. Why not just give herself up?"

"I agree, those are all very valid points. But the fact of the matter is it's extremely incriminating for Mrs. Aguirre," Detective Brewer said. "Keep digging into it. What else have you found out?"

"Celine says she was leaving her house about the time of the murder and that security cameras outside her apartment should be able to verify that," Brigid said. "There's also another employee who may have been disgruntled that the victim was getting a promotion over him."

Detective Brewer nodded. "I'll get a copy of that security footage. Why don't you go talk to that employee?" He looked at his watch. "The guy in the photo's name is Larry Barelli. He's the bartender over at El Lobo, which is just a few blocks away. Pretty much in walking distance. If you can go over there when you're done here and see what he was up to this morning, that would be great. In the meantime, I'll tell my officers to keep an eye out for him. Go ahead and send me that photo. I'll give you a call if the security footage tells us anything."

Brigid nodded. "Will do."

Detective Brewer turned and walked out of the room, leaving Brigid and Linc alone in the office.

"Something isn't adding up," Linc pointed out. "Why would she consent to a search if she knew the gun was in her car?"

"I agree," Brigid said. "And Charlie is either out of practice, or she was telling the truth. If she was, the police just arrested an innocent woman."

"Then I guess it's a good thing we're helping. Let's see what else we can dig up." Linc said. "If she's innocent, we can't let her go to prison. Especially if we're the only ones who can help her."

"What happened to the guy that didn't want to get involved?" Brigid asked playfully.

"That was before there was a chance an innocent woman could go down for murder. If she really did do it, she deserves it. But if she didn't, we have to find out who the real killer is," he said.

"You're right," Brigid said as she put her hand on the door. "Now, let's get out there and ask a few more questions."

CHAPTER SIXTEEN

As they stepped out of the office, Linc caught the attention of one of the remaining officers who hadn't left yet. They'd been standing around talking rather than leaving with most of the other officers.

"Excuse me," Linc said. "Can you tell me where the tour guides are waiting?"

The closest officer, who looked to be a little more seasoned, gave them both the once over. He seemed to be about ready to ask them what business it was of theirs when he noticed Charlie. Once he saw the leash, his skepticism disappeared.

"Is that old Charlie, the lie detector?" he asked with a grin. He squatted down and began to scratch the dog.

"Yes, it is," Brigid said. "We're sort of his handlers for this case."

"Just head down this hall," he said gesturing. "There's a break room down there, third door on the right. It's the one with a glass door. You'll see people sitting inside it. Everyone should be in there."

"Thank you," Linc said.

Heading in the direction the officer had pointed, Charlie trotted along beside Brigid as if he were having the time of his life. Linc apparently noticed it too.

"If I didn't know any better, I'd swear Charlie was smiling," he said with a grin.

Brigid looked down at the dog and thought the same. The corners of his mouth were curled up and his tongue was hanging out happily. "I think you're right. Maybe he isn't as much of a fan of retirement as John had hoped he'd be."

They reached the door and Linc put his hand on the knob. "Maybe he just misses getting out and seeing people. Who knows?" He pushed the door open and all eyes in the room turned towards them. Brigid saw an older man sitting in the back corner with a newspaper. He sipped his coffee nonchalantly, and returned to his paper after seeing them enter.

"Jerry Martinez?' Brigid asked. The older man looked up with surprise.

"Yes?" he asked. Everyone else tried to look as though they weren't interested and failed miserably.

"Would you please step outside so we can talk to you for a moment?" she asked politely. He folded his paper and took one more sip of coffee before standing up and making his way toward them. As they stepped back into the wide hall, Linc looked down both sides to make sure they were alone. The only thing in the hall besides them were a few potted plants and a couple of wooden benches.

"How can I help you?" Jerry asked.

Brigid motioned towards one of the benches and the two of them sat down while Linc stood behind Brigid. "My name is Brigid and this is my husband, Linc. We're working with the police investigators, trying to help them with what happened here this morning," she explained.

"It's a shame what happened to Mark," Jerry began, "but that boy was a mess." He shook his head and looked down at his wrinkled hands.

"What do you mean?" Brigid asked, curious.

"Well, please understand that most of this is speculation. You know how co-workers talk. It's inevitable." He wrung his hands as he looked at the floor, almost as if he didn't want to look Brigid in the eye.

"People had been talking about him having an affair with the boss. He'd also been seen getting cozy with one of the girls from the gift shop." He finally looked up. "And then there were also stories that he had a gambling problem."

Brigid nodded. "Is that so? What made people say that?"

The older man sighed. "Well the kid used to have a pretty decent car, always ate lunch with the other employees, things like that. But lately he started looking a little rough around the edges, and then one day he came to work on the bus. He told everyone he was just cutting back on expenses, but he stopped buying lunch and even tried to borrow money from a few of us."

"Maybe he was down on his luck?" Linc suggested. "Like he'd gotten behind on his bills or something."

"That's what I assumed at first, too," Jerry agreed. "But then I overheard him on the phone talking with someone. He sounded really worried. From what I gathered, it sounded like he owed somebody money, but he was still trying to place a bet. He could have been trying to get in on a poker game or something like that, too. I wasn't totally sure. To be honest, my hearing's not what it used to be." He said the last part almost as if it were an apology.

"That's okay, don't worry about it. You're being very helpful," Brigid said. "Did you happen to catch a name?"

Jerry seemed to think for a moment before he finally spoke. "I'm pretty sure he called the guy Bob."

"Can you tell me where you were this morning between 6:30 and 7:00?" Brigid asked.

Jerry's eyes went wide. "Am I a suspect?"

Brigid smiled reassuringly. "We're just checking at this point. Trying to set up a timeline and all that."

"I was at home, probably sitting at the table eating my breakfast," he said.

"Can anyone vouch for you?" she asked as she wrote down his alibi.

"Yeah, my wife. We were watching the morning news. I even waved to my neighbor when I left the house a little after 7:30," he said. "Should I call them?"

"No, no. That's not necessary. Like I said, we're just making sure we cross everyone off the list. That's all. Doesn't sound like you had a grudge against Mark, did you?" she asked.

"If you're asking if I liked the guy, the answer is no. I don't like so-called men that string more than one woman along. Especially when one of them is married. It's just scummy. Plus, I think he was only having an affair with Celine to get a promotion."

"Can you tell me a little about that?" Brigid questioned. "Like why you would think that?"

"It wasn't long after we heard that one guy here was retiring that it seemed as though Mark started hanging around Celine more than usual. You know, making her laugh and being slightly flirty. I thought something was fishy right from the start.

"I found out from Celine that Mark was going to get the promotion. Looks like it worked. That guy was one of the worst guides we ever had here. He didn't know his stuff like most of us do, which is kind of a requirement when it comes to being the lead." He shrugged. "But I'm over it now."

"You don't care that you were passed over for the promotion?" Linc asked.

Jerry looked up at him. "Oh, sure, I was angry at first. But after I talked with my wife that evening, she pointed out that maybe it was a blessing in disguise. The job has more pay but longer hours. Plus, I'd have to work every other weekend, and that's when we get to see the grandkids. In the end, it probably was for the best."

Brigid nodded. "Maybe it was. Thank you so much, Jerry. You've been a big help." They each shook his hand, and he went back into the break room.

"Well, Charlie didn't move again, so I guess we can assume all of what he told us is correct," Linc said as he joined Brigid on the bench.

"Yeah, I guess so," she said, deep in thought. She tapped her pen against her teeth as she tried to connect the dots.

"What's up?" Linc asked. "You look a little frustrated."

"It's just that it doesn't feel right. Of course, we still have another person to talk to," she said with a sigh, "but it's starting to look like Celine did it."
"Why do you say that?" Linc asked as he petted Charlie.

"Well, think about it. She admitted to finding out that Mark was seeing Zoey. Maybe that was after she gave him a promotion. What if she really had feelings for him, went out on a limb to give him that promotion despite there being better qualified people, only to find out he was seeing someone else?"

Brigid still didn't think it felt like a reason for murder, and Celine didn't seem to be lying, but she could just be good at it. After all, there were people who could pass lie detector tests. Maybe that's why Charlie believed her.

"I don't know, Brigid. Maybe there's something we're missing," Linc said. "I think we should go talk to that bartender and see what he has to say. Although if he's the muscle for some bookie who wants his money, we're going to have to tread lightly. We don't want some kingpin thinking we're nosing around asking questions about his illegal gambling operation."

Linc looked a little apprehensive and Brigid couldn't help but feel the same way. She only hoped she hadn't taken on more than she should have on their honeymoon.

"I know, but we really don't have much choice at this point. Come on, it's probably late enough that the place is open by now. We'll walk over and pretend we're locals" she suggested.

Linc pulled out his phone and typed in the name of the bar on the GPS. "Looks like it's close by. Okay, let's get it over with. Then we can hand the information over to the detective and get back to our honeymoon."

CHAPTER SEVENTEEN

Brigid and Linc began following the GPS's directions toward the bar called El Lobo. Charlie seemed happy to go for a walk along the busy street, trotting smartly along beside them. They hadn't gotten far when Brigid's phone began to ring. She answered it and was surprised to hear Detective Brewer on the other end.

"Brigid, where are you?" he asked.

"We're heading over to El Lobo to speak to the bartender, why?" She stopped walking, and Linc looked at her with a questioning look.

"Scratch that for now. Is Charlie with you?"

"Yes, but I'm not sure if he's still got his talent. He didn't think Celine was lying," she began.

"I want to test him out. Head back to the Alamo. I'm going to have an officer bring you to the station. I have the bartender here for questioning. To be honest, I could just hook him up to a poly, but I don't trust them as much as I trust Charlie. I've seen him pick up lies that the machine didn't detect. Can you do that for me?"

"Of course," Brigid said as she looked at Linc. "We'll see you in a little while."

"Who was that?" Linc asked.

"That was Detective Brewer. He has the bartender down at the station. He wants us to go back to the Alamo and get a ride with one of his officers who will take us to the station. We're to meet him there. He wants to run a test on Charlie," she explained.

They turned around and walked back to the Alamo where they saw an officer leaning up against his squad car. When they approached him, he straightened up and smiled at them.

"Are you Brigid?" he asked after carefully looking at Brigid and the dog. Detective Brewer must have given the officer their description.

"Yes, I am. Are you the officer Detective Brewer sent to give us a ride to the station?" she asked.

"One and the same. Let's get you loaded up, and we'll head on down to the station. My name is Officer Shelby," The young man said. He extended his hand toward Brigid.

"Brigid Olsen. This is my husband, Linc, and this is Charlie," she said by way of an introduction.

Officer Shelby turned and opened the door to the squad car for them. "We better get going. Detective Brewer doesn't like to wait."

Brigid nodded and they climbed into the back of the car. Charlie sat between Brigid and Linc, panting happily. As the officer climbed behind the wheel, Brigid couldn't help but look around at everything inside the squad car. Linc was leaning forward slightly, trying to see over the seat.

"You've got a lot of stuff up there," he said to the officer. "A lot more than I would have expected."

"That I do," Officer Shelby said good-naturedly. "It was pretty overwhelming the first time I saw it all. I honestly didn't know how I would remember everything, plus trying to manage it while I was driving."

"I can only imagine how you must have felt," Linc said. He looked like he'd just won the lottery. "I know it's a long shot, but could you turn on the siren and go really fast?" he asked excitedly. Brigid gave him a dirty look. She didn't care how well trained the officer was, she did not want to drive fast through these streets, siren or not.

Officer Shelby laughed. "I wish I could, but I could get in real trouble if someone reported me. Let alone if we happened to get in a collision or something like that. There are waivers and stuff that have to be signed for ride-alongs."

"Well, that's a bummer," Linc said as he sat back in his seat. Then, his eyes grew wide. "Are you saying I could sign a waiver and do a ride-along?"

"If you got special permission," the officer said. "But they don't grant it very often."

"Man, you're killing my dreams here, Officer Shelby," Linc muttered.

"Sorry," Officer Shelby said apologetically. "I gotta' follow protocol."

"I understand," Linc said sadly. Then he brightened. "When we get to the station do you think we could take a few pictures? It'll be really quick. Maybe you can make it look like you're arresting me?"

Brigid gaped at her husband in surprise. "Seriously?" she asked, shocked.

"Hey, why not? It's not every day you get to ride in the back of a cop car," he shrugged.

Brigid shook her head while Officer Shelby laughed. "Now that we can do. Are you two from around here?" he asked.

"No," Brigid said. "We're here on our honeymoon."

"Oh, that's even better. Where's home?" he asked as they continued through the busy city streets.

"Cottonwood Springs, Colorado," Brigid supplied.

"Well, congratulations. So Linc, you want to let people back home think you got into some trouble while you were on your honeymoon in San Antonio?" he asked with a chuckle.

"Why not?" Linc asked with a shrug as he looked over at Brigid. "Might as well make it as memorable as possible."

Officer Shelby tossed his head back as he laughed loudly. "You know," he said after he recovered himself. "I'm glad I was the one picked to escort you to the station. You guys are a great couple. We're almost there, it's just down the road here." He pointed at a tall building that was much larger than Brigid had expected.

"That's it?" she asked. "It's much bigger than I expected, although I guess I should have known better."

"This is just the PD for our county. There are eight counties that make up San Antonio," he explained. "We divide the city and keep an eye on our little area. Of course, we help the others when needed, but we all try to do what we can in our own area." Officer Shelby seemed proud of that fact and Brigid couldn't blame him. San Antonio was a big place, so of course it would take more than one station to handle it all.

They pulled into the parking lot and Charlie seemed to recognize where they were. He began to whine and dance a little in the seat as if he was ready to jump out of the car and greet everyone.

"That's right, Charlie's an old police dog, isn't he? Now I remember Detective Brewer saying something about him," Officer

Shelby said as they pulled into a parking spot.

"That's right," Brigid said. "He's helping us with our suspects on this murder investigation."

"Good, I know it's an important case. Here, let me open the door for you." He pulled open the door and they climbed out.

"About these pictures," Officer Shelby said. "You want me to put you in handcuffs?" he asked Linc.

"That would be awesome!" Linc said, sounding like a teenage boy.

"Oh, Lord," Brigid said, shaking her head. She couldn't help but smile though. She could tell Linc was having the time of his life. She pulled out her phone as Officer Shelby quickly put Linc in handcuffs. When she looked up again, both the officer and Linc looked like two little boys playing cops and robbers.

She laughed and shook her head. She snapped a few photos, and even got one of Linc getting the handcuffs put on as well as one when he was leaning over against the squad car.

"Make it look like I did something really bad," Linc said. He was doing his best to not look happy when she was taking the pictures, but he was having a time of it.

"I can take my baton out and make it look like I'm holding you down with it," Officer Shelby suggested.

"Oh, yeah. You can kind of press my face into the back of the car, too. Good idea," Linc said eagerly. They got into position and Brigid snapped the picture.

"Are you done now, Linc?" she asked trying to hide her amusement.

"Can I get one more where I'm sitting in the back with the handcuffs on?" he asked. Officer Shelby opened the car door and eased him in the back. Brigid snapped a few more photos. Lastly, Linc looked out the window as if he had really been arrested. When she gave him the thumbs up and Officer Shelby opened the door again, his smile returned.

"How did they look?" he asked. "Were they believable?"

"For the most part," Brigid admitted. "Except for a few where you were grinning like you'd just won the lottery."

"That's because I pretty much did," he said as Officer Shelby removed the handcuffs. "Thanks. That was like winning the lottery and getting a free trip to Disneyland, all in one."

"It was pretty fun," Officer Shelby said, "but we probably better go inside. Detective Brewer will be waiting for you. I don't really need him telling my C.O. that I took too long."

Brigid pulled the leash from her arm where she'd looped it while she was taking pictures. "You won't get in trouble for it, will you?" she asked as they walked toward the building.

"No, it's fine. They give you a little leeway for traffic and such. We should be fine. I'll take you to where Detective Brewer is, and then I'll have to head back out," he said as they reached the front doors of the building.

"Well, if you do get in any trouble, just blame it on me. Tell them I got car sick or something. I can't have you getting in trouble over a little harmless fun," Linc said as they stepped inside the police station.

The ground floor of the police station was bustling with so much activity it almost overwhelmed them. Brigid saw there were more officers in uniform walking around in the room than there were in the entire sheriff's department in Cottonwood Springs, to say nothing of the ones out on patrol or at home with their family.

"Right this way," Officer Shelby said as he led them through the crowd.

CHAPTER EIGHTEEN

After being given visitors badges letting everyone know they were allowed to go farther into the police station, Officer Shelby led them to a smaller area with fewer officers in uniform and more in plainclothes. There were desks and areas that looked like cubicles scattered around the room, surprising Brigid with how ordinary it all seemed.

For some reason she'd expected something a little more like what they showed on television. State-of-the-art technology and modern furniture. Instead, everything looked as though they could be anywhere. Not deep in the heart of a San Antonio police station.

Detective Brewer stood up from a desk in the back and waved them over.

"There he is. Good luck, folks," Officer Shelby said.

"Thank you so much for everything," Linc said as he shook his hand before the officer turned and headed back to where they had come from. Brigid and Linc walked to where Detective Brewer was waiting for them.

"I'm glad you're here. So you aren't sure if Charlie is still up to par, huh?" he asked.

"I don't know. Have you heard anything back about Celine's security camera footage?" Brigid asked as they followed him through a set of grey double doors.

"Not yet, but I should be hearing something any time now. I set up a fake interrogation to test Charlie," Detective Brewer explained as they followed him down the hall. "I've left a few questions on the table for you to ask, and the officer has been instructed to lie when she answers a couple of them. We'll see if Charlie picks up on it. Just make sure you ask all of them, and we'll make sure he's still up to snuff."

"Good idea," Linc commented.

"Linc, you and I are going to be behind a one-way glass mirror watching them. Brigid, you and Charlie go in here. They're waiting for you," Detective Brewer said.

Brigid pushed the door open and was impressed by how realistic the whole scene looked. There was an officer in uniform standing in the corner while a woman, roughly in her thirties, was handcuffed to a table in the middle of the room. She was dressed in jeans and a t-shirt. What looked like a large mirror was at the far end of the room.

"Good afternoon," Brigid said. "My name's Brigid, and this is Charlie."

The woman looked up at her, staying in character. "Just ask your questions. I don't need any nicey-nice small talk," she said sourly.

It gave Brigid pause, but she realized that it probably needed to look as realistic as possible. She pulled out the chair across from the table and took a seat. Giving a cursory glance at the questions, Brigid began. "I see your name is Britney Estevez," she said.

"Yep, sure is," the woman said.

"And you've been at your current job for five years?" Brigid asked.

"Actually six," Britney corrected.

"I see," Brigid commented. "So where were you yesterday around 8:00 p.m.?"

"I was out with my girls. We were partying, because it was my birthday," she began. Just then, Brigid felt a cold wet nose nudge her hand that had been resting on her leg. She looked down at Charlie who was clearly trying to get her attention.

"And was that where you saw your boyfriend with another woman?" Brigid asked as she read the next question.

"Sure was," Britney said as she jutted her chin in the air. Charlie began to really whine then. He obviously knew she was lying. Brigid felt relieved to know the dog still possessed his remarkable talents, but what did that mean?

The police arrested Celine because the murder weapon was in her car. Did someone plant it there? There were no other suspects besides the bartender and as far as Brigid knew, he didn't know Celine. She shook herself back to the present, realizing she still had one more question to read.

"And what did you have for breakfast this morning?" Brigid asked.

"A bowl of apple cinnamon oatmeal with a glass of orange juice and a banana on the side," she said. Brigid turned to look at Charlie who was sitting completely still and quiet. Obviously, she hadn't lied about that one, either.

"Thank you for your time," Brigid said as she stood up. The woman at the table gave her a small apologetic smile, and Brigid returned it with one of her own. She didn't take the scene personally. The woman was just doing what needed to be done. As she stepped back out into the hall, Detective Brewer and Linc were waiting nearby.

"Well, it looks as though Charlie still has it in him," the detective said. "He got each one right. I feel confident enough that I want to take him to speak with our next suspect."

"But that means Celine wasn't lying," Linc offered before Brigid could say anything. "He didn't move a muscle when we spoke to her."

"You're probably right, but I would have been remiss in my duties if I hadn't arrested her when the possible murder weapon was found in her vehicle. It wasn't enough to clear her based on the fact Charlie didn't think she was lying. He may be excellent at his job, but we didn't know at the time if he was still in practice," he explained.

Brigid understood his logic. They had to go by the cold hard facts and not the hunches of a dog in a police investigation. Still, Charlie had proven himself.

"Let's move on to Larry Barelli. He's the bartender from El Lobo. With Charlie here, this shouldn't take too long." He turned to Linc. "You can watch through the mirror like we did in the other room," he said as they walked towards the interrogation room. "It'll be located in about the same place as the last one. I'm sure you'll be able to find it."

He turned to Brigid, "You're going to go into the interrogation room with me. I'll ask the questions, and you keep an eye on Charlie." They stopped outside a room and Detective Brewer pushed the door open.

Inside was a similar set-up like the one Brigid had just left, but knowing this one was real made her a bit more nervous. She looked at the man sitting at the table. He wasn't handcuffed, probably because he wasn't under arrest. Still, the thought she might be sitting down across from a murderer made her nervous.

"Good afternoon, Mr. Barelli," Detective Brewer began. "I'm Detective Brewer, and this is my associate, Brigid, as well as K-9 officer Charlie. Do you have anything to say before I ask you a few questions?"

"No," the man's low voice rumbled. "But I have to be at work a little before 7:00 tonight," he said as he eyed Charlie.

"As long as everything goes well, that shouldn't be a problem. Do you mind if we get started?" the detective asked.

"Not at all," the man said. Brigid found herself fidgeting with the leash, nervously awaiting the questions.

"Do you know a man by the name of Mark Muller?" Detective Brewer began.

"I may have heard his name before," Larry said. "What about him?"

Charlie seemed to want to move, but didn't. Brigid wondered what that meant.

"Well, it looks like you've probably done more than just heard his name," the detective said as he opened a folder. He slid a printed version of the photo Brigid had gotten from Celine showing Larry and Mark having a conversation across the table. "This looks like you having a conversation with him."

"Yeah, okay. We talked once," the man admitted.

"The person who took this picture felt as though you were being rather intimidating when you spoke to Mark. They said he was pretty distracted and upset after you two talked. Care to tell me why?"

"I- I-," Larry began. He seemed to be conflicted as to what he should say. Finally, he let out a sigh. "Look, I'm not really sure I can tell you. It's not that I don't want to. I'm sure you wouldn't be asking if it wasn't important. But it's, I guess you could say, a conflict of interest."

"Mark is dead, Larry. He was murdered this morning at the

Alamo. If you don't start explaining, you might go down for it. Is that what you want?" Detective Brewer pushed. He pulled out a crime scene photo of Mark and placed it in front of Larry. "If you're in trouble, we can help. But you have to help us first. What do you know about this?"

Larry looked shocked. He couldn't seem to tear his eyes away from the photo of Mark's dead body. Finally, he shook his head and looked up at the detective. "I think they might hurt me if they know I said anything to you," he stammered.

"Nobody's going to know. Hundreds of people go in and out of this building every day," Detective Brewer said easily. He leaned forward. "Who are you afraid of?"

"I met this guy while I was working late one night. It was a little slower than usual, and he approached me. Said I looked like the kind of guy his boss could use if I needed to earn a little extra cash. He sold it to me like I'd be doing something like security work, you know? I called the number. Supposedly the guy's name is Bob," he explained.

Detective Brewer nodded. "I've heard of him. Go on."

"He told me that some people owed him money and all I needed to do was be the guy who went out and collected it. He explained he doesn't get out a lot and that he needed reliable people to do this sort of thing for him.

"At first, I didn't know. I swear I didn't. I don't know why I didn't put two and two together, but I didn't. I've only collected from a couple of people, and I never laid a finger on any of them. He sent me to tell Mark he was expecting the money he owed him to be paid. That's all."

Detective Brewer looked over at Brigid and Charlie, who was still sitting quietly. Apparently, Larry was telling the truth.

Detective Brewer nodded. "I understand. Did you see Mark after that?"

"No," Larry said shaking his head emphatically. "But Bob did tell me to meet up with him again and tell Mark it was time to pay up or else. I just hadn't gotten around to it yet."

"I see," the detective said thoughtfully. "And where were you this morning between 6:30 and 7:00 a.m.?"

"I was at the diner over on East Street having breakfast. I flirted with the waitress and gave her my number," he said with wide eyes.

With Charlie sitting so still, Brigid was sure Larry was telling the truth. That only meant one thing; they'd run out of suspects. She was starting to wonder if maybe it really had been a random shooting. After all, who else could have done it?

"Thank you," Detective Brewer said. "I need you to stay a little longer so we can get your written statement." He stood up and headed toward the door. Brigid and Charlie followed. Once they were out in the hall, Detective Brewer sighed. "Well that didn't help the case at all."

"No, it didn't," Brigid said shaking her head. "That means we had to have missed someone or this was just a random act of violence."

"It's not random," he said. "Whoever did this was close. Almost point blank. We're missing something."

Linc joined them in the hall. "Looks like he didn't do it," he began, "but I had a thought. What if we're going about this all wrong?"

"What do you mean?" Brewer asked.

"Well, Celine didn't do it, but the murder weapon was in her car, right?" he asked.

"Correct," Detective Brewer said.

"That means it had to be someone who knew her. Someone who'd want to see her go down for the murder," Linc supplied.

"Are you saying it was Zoey? But she has an alibi," Brigid said.

"No, I was thinking more along the lines of Celine's husband. She said she's married. What if her husband found out she was cheating on him with Mark?" Linc asked. "Plus, he'd have a key to Celine's car and could use it to unlock her car and stash the gun in it."

"That's brilliant," Detective Brewer said. "We need to get him down here. I'll get some officers on it. Wait right here. I want Charlie with us when we talk to Celine," he said before rushing off.

CHAPTER NINETEEN

"We have the surveillance footage. One of my guys looked it over and Celine wasn't lying, she left home at the time she said. But while I was at it, I had him look to see what time her husband left this morning. He left their home around 5:00 a.m., plenty of time to make it to the Alamo and meet up with Mark. I have a couple of officers heading to his office right now to bring him in for questioning," Detective Brewer said when he returned to where Brigid and Linc were waiting.

"Now what?" Brigid asked.

"You and I do the same thing we just did, only with Celine. We're going to see what else she may have to say." He turned to Linc. "Same as before, just a different room."

Linc nodded. "Gotcha."

Detective Brewer took them farther down the hall, turned a corner, and stopped outside another room. "Here we are," he said as he pushed the door open.

When they entered, Celine was handcuffed to the table and her head hung low. She didn't even look up as they took their seats.

"Well, Mrs. Aguirre, I have some good news for you," Detective

Brewer said. She looked up at him, and Brigid was shocked by the physical state she was in. She could hardly believe it was the same woman she'd spoken to earlier that day. Her makeup was almost completely gone, probably cried off. Her red-rimmed eyes looked lost and broken. He pulled out a key and undid the handcuffs. "We know you weren't the one who murdered Mark."

The woman's face completely changed. She went from sullen to gratefully sobbing. "Oh, thank goodness," she cried. "I told you I didn't do it."

"Yes, you did. But you do understand what it looked like." He signaled to another officer who was holding a box. The officer brought it over to the detective and he lifted the lid, pulling out a pistol which was inside a plastic evidence bag. "Have you ever seen this gun before?"

Celine had been busy rubbing her wrists. She stopped and looked at what he was holding. She squinted slightly before leaning forward. "That looks like the one we have in our safe at home," she said.

"I see. Actually, this is yours. It's registered to your husband, a Dr. William Aguirre. Did you know it wasn't in your home?"

She shook her head. "No. I didn't want him to get the thing in the first place. He wanted to keep it in his nightstand, but I insisted he keep it locked in the safe. I couldn't sleep knowing it was next to him in the bedroom." Realization seemed to set in. "This is the murder weapon?" she asked wide-eyed.

"Yes, ma'am. It is," Brewer confirmed. "We got the ballistics test back. It's definitely the gun that was used to kill Mark Muller."

"But how? The only ones who know the combination to the safe are my husband and me," she said but even as she said it, her eyes grew dark. "Did William kill Mark?"

"We're unsure at this point in time. I have a couple of officers out looking for him right now with orders to bring him in for questioning," he said.

"He should be at work. He's supposed to work a 12-hour shift at the hospital today," she said. "But surely he didn't do this."

"We don't know. We checked the surveillance footage you pointed us to and it shows him leaving with more than enough time to commit the murder. All we have are theories at this point," he admitted.

"But I don't understand," Celine said shaking her head. "He never came to my work. To my knowledge he never met Mark. I don't see how he could have found out I was having an affair with Mark."

Detective Brewer shrugged. "I don't know, but you've confirmed that this is your husband's and your gun. Only you two have the combination to the safe where it's kept. It's all circumstantial at this point, but you're a smart woman. I'm sure you can see what we're seeing."

A knock on the door made them all turn towards it. An officer in uniform stepped inside and apologized. "I'm sorry for interrupting, Detective," she said. "But we have Dr. Aguirre in interrogation room number two."

"Thank you," he said. He turned to Celine. "If you'd like, I can put you in a safe area so you can see what he has to say," he said. "He won't be able to see you, but you'll be able to see him."

She turned toward the mirror as if she just realized what it was for. As she stared at it, a mix of emotions played out across her face. Finally, she turned back to him and nodded. "Yes, please."

With one quick nod he stood up and the officer in the corner stepped forward. Detective Brewer placed the gun back in the box and carried it with him as he left the room. As they exited the room, Linc joined them.

"Please take Linc and Mrs. Aguirre to where they can view the interrogation," he instructed the officer.

He led both of them away, but Detective Brewer put his hand on Brigid's arm to get her to stay back. "This one may go much differently. If you'd like, I can take Charlie, but it would probably be better if you took him in the room since he seems quite attached to you. I don't mind having you in there, but if you don't feel comfortable..." He let his sentence hang in the air between them.

"No, I can do this," Brigid insisted. "I want to go in."

"Are you sure?" he asked. "This guy is more than likely our killer. He could be capable of anything."

"I'm sure," Brigid nodded. "I've dealt with this before."

"Okay," Detective Brewer said. "Let's go speak with the good doctor."

He turned and led Brigid and Charlie down the hall. He opened a nearby door, and they went into another interrogation room.

The man at the table looked nothing like what Brigid had expected. When you suspect that someone's a murderer, but you've never seen them, your mind automatically thinks of someone who looks like Larry Barelli, a big guy who looks like he's angry at the world. Instead, Dr. Aguirre looked like an academic. His salt and pepper short hair and thin wire frame glasses fit that description. He was still wearing his white doctor's coat.

"Thank you for meeting with me, Dr. Aguirre," Detective Brewer said after introducing everyone. "I just have a few questions for you. I hope we aren't interrupting anything important."

"Not at all," the doctor said. "I was told you may need my assistance on a case?" He looked pleasant and mildly interested, as if he was out for a casual walk in the neighborhood and not in an interrogation room.

"Yes, I do," Detective Brewer said. He opened the box and pulled out the same gun he'd shown Celine a short time earlier. Dr. Aguirre's mild interest fell away, and was replaced by a blank look. Brigid watched his face to see if he would react, but nothing happened. She wondered if this was the face he put on for his patients when he had to give them bad news.

"Do you recognize this gun, sir?" the detective asked.

"Well, it looks a lot like one my wife and I have at home," he began. "We keep it locked in a safe."

"I see," Brewer said. "And do you know a man named Mark Muller?"

Something flashed across the doctor's face so quickly Brigid wondered if she'd imagined it. It was there and gone, almost in the blink of an eye. "No, I'm afraid I don't."

Charlie began bumping Brigid's hand insistently. Detective Brewer looked over and saw the dog's movement before looking up at Brigid. She gave a small nod, and he turned back to Dr. Aguirre.

"Well, it seems your wife does. He worked at the Alamo with her and somehow wound up being murdered this morning. Whoever did it used this weapon," the detective explained.

The stony expression on Dr. Aguirre's face remained in place. "Are you saying my wife killed one of her co-workers?" he asked.

"Not exactly," Brewer said as he leaned back in his chair. "You see, we have evidence that she was still at home at the time of the murder. But you weren't."

There was no sound and tension filled the room as they waited for his response. Brigid could hear the blood that was pulsing through her veins.

"I went to work early this morning. I told her when I left," the doctor finally said.

"Yes," Brewer agreed. "But your shift didn't actually start until much later, which we have confirmation of from the hospital."

"So I went in early?" Dr. Aguirre shrugged. "That's not a crime."

Charlie gave a slight whimper.

"Are you're telling me that you went straight from your house to the hospital and started an early shift?" Detective Brewer asked.

"Precisely," he said confidently.

Charlie began to whine and nudge at Brigid more insistently.

"Then why does the hospital surveillance camera footage show you not coming in until a little after 8:00 this morning?"

The doctor seemed surprised that they'd checked that fact out already. His cool demeanor slipped a little, and his face flushed. "Okay, I may have fibbed a bit. I stopped somewhere for a bite to eat." Charlie whined even louder now.

"Where did you go?" Detective Brewer asked as he leaned forward in his seat.

Brigid knew where this was going. He was letting the doctor talk himself into a corner.

"I grabbed a breakfast burrito at a drive-thru," he huffed. Charlie began to wiggle and whine while bumping Brigid insistently. Dr. Aguirre turned and looked at Brigid. "Miss, I believe your dog needs to use the restroom."

"Actually, he doesn't," interrupted the detective. "He's a highly trained police dog, and he does that when someone isn't telling the truth. Now doctor, would you like to tell me what really happened?"

Dr. Aguirre looked utterly shocked. He looked down at Charlie who was sitting still and then he looked at Brigid. She saw the fear in his eyes as he realized he was cornered with nowhere to go. Then abruptly, his face became one of resignation.

"Okay, I admit it. I killed him," he sighed.

"Excuse me?" Detective Brewer said.

"I said I killed Mark Muller," the doctor said much more loudly. "I showed up with our gun hoping to scare him. I found out he was having an affair with my wife, and I wanted him out of the picture. I knew something was up with her. She started singing when she'd cook dinner and get a distant happy look in her eyes.

"When I asked her what was going on, she'd say it was nothing, so I followed her. One time when I sat in my car in the Alamo parking lot around the time she got off work, I saw him get in the car with her. I followed them and they parked in a secluded area. I knew what they were doing. I'm no fool."

"Tell us what happened this morning, Dr. Aguirre," the detective said.

"I showed up at the Alamo dressed all in black. I thought if I scared him maybe he'd quit his job or something. I didn't really have a plan. When he saw me, he lunged at me and started to defend himself. He was surprisingly strong. I started to get worried that my plan was not working as I intended. Sometime during the struggle the gun went off. That's when he was shot," he explained.

"Are you saying it was an accident?" Brewer asked.

"Yes, sir. I didn't go there with the intention to kill him. I just wanted him to leave my wife alone."

"If that's so, how did the murder weapon end up in her car?" Detective Brewer asked.

Dr. Aguirre sighed. "It was a moment of weakness. I didn't see why I should have to go to prison since it was her fault it happened. It was because of her infidelity. If she hadn't cheated, none of this would have happened in the first place, so I planted the gun in her car. I had a key to her car, so I unlocked the trunk and put it in there."

"Dr. William Aguirre, you are under arrest for the murder of Mark Muller. Anything you say can and will be used against you in a court of law. If you cannot afford an attorney, one will be provided for you. Do you understand the rights I've just read to you?" he asked as the officer in the room put the doctor in handcuffs.

"Yes, I do," he said, sounding defeated. "Would someone call my wife and let her know what's happened?"

"Don't worry, she already knows," the detective told him.

"But how?" he asked, looking stricken.

"When we found the gun in her car she was placed under arrest. I let her go shortly before coming in here to question you. She's heard our entire conversation," he explained. "Actually, she's located behind that mirror on the wall and is listening to our conversation right now."

"I'm sorry," Dr. Aguirre began. "I'm sorry, my love. I know I wasn't the best husband to you, but when I saw you with Mark, I went mad. I couldn't stand the thought of another man touching you," he cried out as he was led out of the interrogation room.

In a few moments, the officer who had taken Celine and Linc to the observation room brought them in. Celine was crying once again.

"He's right, it's all my fault," she sobbed.

"No, it's not," Linc said consolingly. "If he'd been a good husband, you would have felt taken care of and loved. You wouldn't have felt as though you had nothing to lose by having an affair with

Mark." Linc turned to Brigid. "We spoke in the other room for a bit."

Brigid nodded. "There's never an excuse for murder, Celine. You were human, nothing more."

"But he's right. I should have remained faithful. Then none of this would have happened, and Mark would still be alive." Her grief was painful to watch. Not only had she lost her lover, now she'd also lost her husband, both of the same day.

"All you can do now is move forward," Detective Brewer offered. "I know it sounds harsh, but it's true. No amount of 'what ifs' or 'should haves' can change what has happened. Your husband made a choice. Now he's going to have to pay for that choice."

Celine nodded. "I know you're right, but...."

Brigid stood up and moved toward Linc with Charlie. "Detective, it's been a long day. Do you think Linc and I could get a ride back to our car now?"

"Of course," he said. "I'll find someone to give you a ride back to it."

EPILOGUE

Brigid and Linc were sitting in the Japanese Tea Garden, enjoying their surroundings. "I can't believe we managed to get involved in a murder investigation, helped solve it, and still have time for the rest of our honeymoon," Linc marveled.

"Thanks to your quick thinking after we ran out of suspects," Brigid said as she bumped him.

"Aww, shucks," he said pretending to be bashful. "It was nothing."

"Now the killer is behind bars, and we're on our last day here in San Antonio," Brigid said. "Are you ready to head back home after everything that's happened?"

"Honestly? Yes," Linc admitted. "It's been so much fun, and I wouldn't trade it for the world. I've had so many firsts while we were here. First time surfing, first time riding in a police car…"

"First time doing a police ride-along," Brigid said.

Linc broke out into a huge grin. "Exactly. I couldn't believe it when they agreed to let me go on one. When the chief of police called to personally thank us and asked if there was anything he could do in return, I saw my opening."

"As soon as you said the word 'actually' I knew what you were going to ask," Brigid laughed.

"Was it that obvious?" he asked.

"Uh, yeah, to me. I know you too well, Linc Olsen." She leaned over and kissed him.

"This place is much nicer than I thought it would be," Linc admitted. "When you said you wanted to visit some tea garden while we were on our honeymoon, I seriously questioned how interesting it could be."

"I think it's beautiful," Brigid sighed. The large Japanese archways and narrow winding paths made her feel as if she was in some sort of a Japanese fairytale. As she looked around, she began thinking that maybe she could do something similar in her backyard at home. When she told Linc what she was thinking, he laughed loudly.

"Have you forgotten about your horse of a dog?" he asked. "You know all he'd have to do is get the urge to start digging, and it would all be gone."

"Ugh, you're right," Brigid sighed. "Well, maybe someday."

They stood up and began to stroll down one of the garden paths, enjoying their last day in San Antonio.

*****

When they returned to their home in Cottonwood Springs, Brigid and Linc began to sort through the mail that had been delivered while they were away.

"Look at this," Linc said as he uncovered a box. "A package from the San Antonio Police Department." He took out his pocket knife and sliced the tape. Folding back the flaps, he started pulling out multiple items. All of the things in the box were local to San Antonio. A bottle of wine, chocolates, and more food, as well as a beautiful piece of art glass.

"Wow, all this stuff is amazing," Brigid said as she marveled at the glass.

"Look at this!" Linc cried out. He was holding a framed photo of him dressed as an officer standing with Officer Shelby. "Man, that guy was so much fun. I even friended him online."

"Linc! You did not!" Brigid cried out, laughing.

"Sure did. He told me if we ever visit San Antonio again to look him up," he said with a grin.

"I swear, you make friends everywhere you go, don't you?" Brigid said.

Linc shrugged. "I try." He continued to look in the box. "Hey, here's a letter." He pulled it out and handed it to Brigid. In tight, small handwriting an envelope was addressed to both of them. She sliced it open and pulled out the letter.

Dear Brigid and Linc,

I hope the rest of your honeymoon went much better than the day we met. Please don't think that this is what San Antonio is always like. Granted, bad things happen here, but plenty of good happens here, too.

The department put together a nice little 'thank you' package for all your hard work. Each item is made locally in San Antonio. We thought we would send you some of the best things our fine city has to offer, just in case you missed them.

You asked me to let you know how things were going with everyone else from the case. I personally paid them each a visit to find out for you. Celine sends her love, and she even pitched in on the gift box. The swirled glass vase is from her. She says it's art. I don't know about that, but I have to admit, I'm no expert.

She asked that you keep in touch, and I will be adding her email address at the end. She's extremely grateful to you for everything you did and is glad you decided to pick San Antonio for your honeymoon. Otherwise, she's not sure whether or not she'd still be sitting in a jail cell. I reassured her we would have figured it out by now, but she didn't sound very certain that we were capable of it.

Zoey's still working at the gift shop, but she's made plans to start college this fall. She decided life is just too short to put things off, and she's going to study criminal psychology. Hopefully she'll do well and then she can eventually join our department. She has a new fire in her, and she says she wants to make sure the bad guys get caught. She felt badly that she'd accused Celine of murdering Mark, and she was pretty upset that the real killer almost got away.

Jerry got the position as Lead Tour Guide at the Alamo. Now he enjoys his time in his office, and he's off his feet. He's requiring the tour guides to know even more about the history of the Alamo and routinely informs them of anything else he's managed to learn along the way. That guy is seriously dedicated to history.

Larry's been helping us as an informant. We're a few steps closer to taking down the illegal gambling ring his employer 'Bob' runs. We've managed to get a few of the other bigger players, but Bob is still eluding us. We're not worried though. We'll catch him.

Thank you for all of your amazing help. I have to say, you definitely expedited the process for us.

Wishing you all the best,

Detective Brewer

"Does the guy not have a first name or is it 'detective'?" Linc asked.

"I don't know, but this was really nice of them. I can't wait until Holly gets back, so we can tell her everything," Brigid said as she picked up each item and inspected them one by one.

"And what about the whole adoption thing?" Linc asked.

"I want to ask her, but I want to do it in a special way," Brigid said.

"That sounds like a good idea," Linc said as he pulled her into his arms. "You're always full of those."

"Thanks," Brigid said as she kissed him. "I couldn't have done it without you."

RECIPES

RED WINE MUSHROOM SAUCE FOR MEAT

Ingredients:
½ tbsp. cooking oil
½ cup shallots, roughly chopped (White onion will also work.)
1 cup red wine
1 bunch green onions, finely chopped, green part only
¼ cup fresh rosemary, chopped with stems removed
2 tbsp. butter
8 oz. brown mushrooms, stems removed, quartered
1 tbsp. herbs de Provence
1 tbsp. corn starch mixed w/2 tbsp. water to form a slurry

Directions:
Add oil to 12-inch cast iron skillet and heat on med-high until hot. Add shallots and mushrooms and cook 3-4 minutes. Add green onion and cook for 1 minute.

Add wine, increase heat to high and bring to a boil. Reduce volume by ½ (about 3-4 minutes). Add butter, rosemary, and herbs de Provence. Cook 2-3 minutes. Slowly pour slurry into pan until desired thickness of sauce is obtained. Spoon mushroom wine sauce over cooked meat. Enjoy!

GOURMET BEEF STEW

Ingredients:
2 garlic cloves, minced
4 anchovy fillets, rinsed and minced (Available in small tins.)
1 tbsp. tomato paste
4 lb. boneless beef chuck roast, cut into 1 ½-inch chunks
2 tbsp. vegetable oil
1 large onion, halved and sliced
4 carrots, peeled and cut into 1-inch bite size pieces
¼ cup all-purpose flour
2 cups red wine
2 bay leaves
4 sprigs fresh thyme
1 ½ cups frozen pearl onions, thawed
1 cup frozen peas, thawed
Salt and freshly ground pepper to taste

Directions:
Adjust oven rack to lower-middle position and heat oven to 300 degrees. Combine garlic, anchovies, and tomato paste in a small bowl, making a paste. Set aside.

Pat meat dry with paper towels. Heat 1 tbsp. oil in Dutch oven over high heat until it starts to smoke. Add half of beef and cook until well-browned on all sides, about 8 minutes. Transfer beef to a large plate. Repeat with remaining 1 tbsp. oil, leaving second batch of beef in pot after browning.

Reduce heat to medium and return first batch of beef to pot. Stir in onions and carrots and cook until onions are soft, scraping bottom while cooking. Add garlic mixture and cook about 30 seconds.

Add flour and cook, stirring constantly until no dry flour remains, about 30 seconds. Slowly add wine, increase heat to high, and cook until wine is slightly reduced, about 2 minutes. Stir in broth, bay leaves, and thyme. Bring to simmer, cover, transfer to oven and cook for 1 1/2 hours.

Stir in pearl onions and peas. Continue to cook for ½ hour more. Remove bay leaves and discard. Season with salt and pepper to taste. Serve and enjoy!

SHORTBREAD COOKIES WITH DULCE DE LECHE

Ingredients:
8 oz. unsalted butter, room temperature
½ cup sugar + 2 tbsp.
2 cups plain flour
1 can sweetened condensed milk to make dulce de leche

Directions:
Remove paper wrapper from condensed milk can. Place can in a large saucepan on its side. Cover with water and bring to a simmer. Cook for 2 – 3 hours, depending on how dark you want the caramel filling to be (dulce de leche). Remove from pan with tongs and let cool completely before opening can.

Preheat oven to 350 degrees. Line 2 cookie sheets with parchment paper. Combine butter and sugar in a bowl and mix until well combined. Add flour and mix until it looks like dough. Form it into a ball with your hands.

Scatter 2 tbsp. sugar over a work surface and place dough on it. Flatten with your hand until a thickness of about ½ inch. Place a sheet of parchment paper over it and use a rolling pin to lightly roll it to a thickness of about ¼ inch. Cut into rounds with a cookie cutter and place them on cookie sheets. Ball up the excess dough, roll out, and cut more rounds. Makes approximately 16 cookies.

Bake for 15 – 18 minutes until slightly brown on the edges. May appear undercooked, but will continue to cook on the cookie sheets when removed from oven. Cool cookies.

When cookies are cool, spread half of the cookies with a dollop of the dulce de leche. Place the remaining cookies on top, sandwiching them. Enjoy!

PANNA COTTA WITH FRESH BERRIES

Ingredients:
1 cup whole milk
1 tbsp. unflavored powdered gelatin
3 cups whipping cream
1/3 cup honey
1 tbsp. sugar
Pinch salt
2 cups assorted fresh berries

Directions:
Place the milk in a small bowl. Sprinkle the gelatin over it. Let stand 3 – 5 minutes to soften gelatin. Pour mixture into a heavy saucepan and stir over medium heat just to the point the gelatin dissolves but the milk doesn't boil, about 5 minutes. Add the cream, honey, sugar, and salt. Stir until the sugar dissolves, 5 – 7 minutes. Remove from the heat. Pour into wine glasses until about ½ full. Cool slightly, then refrigerate until set, about 6 hours.

When ready to serve, spoon the berries over the panna cotta and enjoy!

JOHN'S CHILI CHEESE OMELET

Ingredients:
Can of chili, with or without beans (I like to use leftover homemade chili.)
3 jumbo eggs, beaten well
1/6 onion, diced
1 tbsp. butter
¼ cup shredded cheese (Your choice.)
Salt and pepper to taste

Optional: 1 jalapeno pepper, first cut in half. Remove seeds and dice

Directions:

In a small saucepan, heat the chili and keep warm. Season the eggs with salt and pepper. Melt butter in a small skillet. Add a little of the onion and jalapeno and cook for about 1 minute. Add eggs all at once and swirl around pan, scraping and tilting edges to cook evenly.

When just slightly moist on top, place about ½ cup warm chili on half of the eggs. Top with shredded cheese and additional onions and jalapeno, if desired. Gently fold the other half of the omelet over to form semicircle.

Slide onto serving plate and top with a spoonful of chili and cheese for presentation. Enjoy!

NOTE: Above ingredients are for each omelet you intend to make. If making more than one omelet, increase the amount of the ingredients proportionally.

Paperbacks & Ebooks for FREE

Go to www.dianneharman.com/freepaperback.html and get your FREE copies of Dianne's books and favorite recipes immediately by signing up for her newsletter.

Once you've signed up for her newsletter you're eligible to win three paperbacks. One lucky winner is picked every week. Hurry before the offer ends!

ABOUT THE AUTHOR

Dianne lives in Huntington Beach, California, with her husband, Tom, a former California State Senator, and her boxer dog, Kelly. Her passions are cooking, reading, and dogs, so whenever she has a little free time, you can either find her in the kitchen, playing with Kelly in the back yard, or curled up with the latest book she's reading.

Her award winning books include:

Cedar Bay Cozy Mystery Series

Cedar Bay Cozy Mystery Series - Boxed Set

Liz Lucas Cozy Mystery Series

Liz Lucas Cozy Mystery Series - Boxed Set

High Desert Cozy Mystery Series

High Desert Cozy Mystery Series - Boxed Set

Northwest Cozy Mystery Series

Northwest Cozy Mystery Series - Boxed Set

Midwest Cozy Mystery Series

Midwest Cozy Mystery Series - Boxed Set

Jack Trout Cozy Mystery Series

Cottonwood Springs Cozy Mysteries

Coyote Series

Midlife Journey Series

Red Zero Series

Black Dot Series

Newsletter

If you would like to be notified of her latest releases please go to www.dianneharman.com and sign up for her newsletter.

Website: www.dianneharman.com,
Blog: www.dianneharman.com/blog
Email: dianne@dianneharman.com

PUBLISHING 4/30/19

MURDER IN PALM SPRINGS

BOOK EIGHT OF

THE HIGH DESERT COZY MYSTERY SERIES

http://getBook.at/Palm

An aging American idol. A murder. A dog with paranormal abilities. Walking to the mailbox can be deadly, but sometimes things aren't what they seem.

Join Marty and her dog, Patron, as they eliminate suspects in the murder of a beloved rock star in Palm Springs, California.

This is book number eight in the bestselling High Desert Cozy Mystery Series by two-time USA Today Bestselling Author Dianne Harman. Enjoy!

Open your smartphone, point and shoot at the QR code below. You will be taken to Amazon where you can pre-order 'Murder in Palm Springs'.

(Download the QR code app onto your smartphone from the iTunes or Google Play store in order to read the QR code below.)